UNTOLD
MAYHEM

Mark Tullius

VINCERE
P R E S S

Published by Vincere Press
65 Pine Ave., Ste 806
Long Beach, CA 90802

Cover design by Michael Squid
Graphic Design by Florencio Ares aresjun@gmail.com

"The Feeling's Back" first published by *Midwest Literary Magazine* 2010
"Left Behind" first published by *Willy Writers* 2010
"Pillow Talk" first published by *Enigma* 2002
"Marked" first published by *Thou Shall Not,* 2006
"Left Unfinished" first published by *Raw Meat* 2006
"Gone for Good" first published by *Murder Hole* 2002
"The Mirror" first published by *Seventh Dimensions* 2007

TABLE OF CONTENTS

In the Cards

This neighborhood is all palm trees and plush lawns, the streets quiet. Kids are at school, adults at work, real jobs making real money, not fifty dollars here and there, maybe a few hundred at a party reading people's fortunes.

I've been sitting here five minutes, but it's ten o'clock, time to perform. My selenite necklace warms my hand as I rub it between my thumb and forefinger. I lock on my eyes in the rear view and tell myself, "Believe." It doesn't matter what anyone else thinks. Doesn't matter what they say. "Just believe."

My smile feels genuine, my eyes a brighter blue. I pick up my purse and hope Jill won't spot it's a knockoff. My silk pouch is in there on top of the yellow pepper spray Fernando insists on. He doesn't doubt my judgment, only my ability to protect myself. It's the same reason he carries his own canister.

With my luck the spray will leak all over my purse, so I toss it into the glovebox. It slides off the yellowed owner's manual and slips beside a sprig of sage. I can't let fear control me.

The glovebox doesn't latch that great anymore and pops right open. I try again and it stays until I shut the car door.

There's no time for this so I head up the driveway, past the Range Rover, the sun sparkling off its dazzling white exterior. My rusty red hatchback's an embarrassment, same one I was so proud of back when I was 18.

I try not to notice the details so they won't cloud my judgment and alter the reading, but it's hard not to. It's bad

1

enough that Jill already told me her husband is a sheriff, but now here's a house we could never afford on Fernando's teaching salary and a car we couldn't lease.

I blow out a deep breath and knock on the door. Heavy thuds approach and a man says, "Just a second."

The man who opens the door is a head taller than me with short brown hair and a crisp blue button-down hugging his muscular frame. He offers his hand and a straight smile. "Gwen? I'm Robbie. Come on in."

"Thank you so much for having me."

The entryway is lined with photos of Robbie and Jill in different locales, drinks in hand in every one. "Jill is the one you should thank. She couldn't stop talking about how amazing you were."

"Well, I'm glad you're up for it. Have you done this before?"

"Virgin." Robbie walks me past the stairs leading down, then points at the mahogany table in the dining room. "Will this work?"

"This is perfect." I pull out the chair that faces the fireplace, set the purse by my feet. "Will Jill be joining us?" I ask Robbie, who has walked into the adjoining kitchen.

Everything in the kitchen is shiny black tile and silver appliances. With his hand on the fridge, Robbie says, "She's out running errands. Sorry, I figured she would've mentioned it in her texts."

I pick up the purse, set it on the table, and take out the pouch. "Oh, it's no problem. I just assumed she'd be here."

He opens the fridge and asks what I'd like. "Got beer, coolers, soda."

"Thanks, but I'm all set."

Robbie walks over with a Corona and says, "Yes, it's early, but I work graveyard and just got off." He picks up a deck of cards from the counter and holds it so I can see the Norse god on the cover. "Should we use these? I just bought them yesterday at a new age store. Man, I felt like a nutcase walking through there."

I smile to hide the hurt and make it seem as if it's a joke when I say, "A feeling I know all too well."

"Oh, I didn't mean anything by it."

"It comes with the territory. Nutcase, certifiable, going to hell, scammer, preying on the weak. Everyone's got their opinion." I almost say something about Fernando not believing, but don't want Robbie judging me and my relationship with my husband.

He sits across from me and drinks from the bottle. "Well I promise you'll get none of that from me."

"That's sweet of you, but we better wait to see how you feel when I'm done." I slip the cards out of the pouch. "And if you don't mind, I'd prefer using my set. The reading will be more accurate."

"Not at all." He nods at the cards. "Are those the ones you used for Jill?"

I shuffle the deck and set it in front of him. "Yep, it's the only one I use. My teacher said to connect with one set and stick with it. So far, so good with this one."

"Like I said, Jill was impressed. She kept taking about it, said we were in for a big change."

His eyes are hard, yet kind, capable of fun. If I had to guess, they'd seen death, but he was still happy and living, not simply surviving. I ask, "Do you have any questions before we start?"

"Do you need these to see my future? I've heard some people can tell what a person is all about just by looking at them."

"One of my friends can see auras, but I've never had that ability. And as for the cards, I'm not predicting your future as much as helping you examine yourself."

"Great, my least favorite activity," he says with a smile.

"Think of it as a dialogue between you and the images and the messages tied to them."

"Got it." Robbie takes another swig of beer. "Do I respond to your answers?"

"It's your session so feel free to do as you like, although you'd probably be more likely to accept truths if you don't feed me any details. We can just let the cards do the talking."

He takes a drink but keeps his eyes on me. "Did Jill tell you anything?"

"It's hard to remember, especially with so many readings one after another. Lots of times the thoughts leave me as soon as the energy changes."

"I'm sure that's a good thing. I wouldn't want to walk around with everyone else's thoughts filling my head."

I hate this part because I know it sounds crazy, but it's something I need to do. "Do you give me permission to access whatever energy comes to me?"

"Absolutely." He takes a quick drink and says, "You haven't been doing it already? Is there an on-off switch?"

"Sort of, but no one can see it." I close my eyes and pray to my guardian angel, ask for guidance and clarity. "If I walked around this open, I'd be a basket case within the week."

"Wow," he says, sounding like he's just being polite.

The house seems colder than it'd been. I would've chalked it up to the air conditioning kicking on if it weren't for the accompanying image of a baseball bat.

"You okay?" he asks. "You shivered."

I say I'm fine. "Did you happen to play baseball?"

"Hey, that's no fair," he says with a smile. "There's my college photo in the hallway."

"That must be it," I say, figuring the photo got picked up by my subconscious. "Alright, if you're ready to do this, please tap the top of the deck three times to clear the energy."

"Like this?"

"You're a natural. Go ahead and shuffle the deck. If there's a question you'd like answered, please think of it now but keep it to yourself."

"Done." Robbie shuffles the cards like a professional poker player and sets them back down.

"Now, one at a time, pick five cards and place them face down. First in the middle, then left, right, below, and above."

With no hesitation, Robbie lays out all five, ignores the thump that sounds like it came from below us.

I point to the first card and say, "This one represents your present situation or your question, something you're dealing with." When I lay my hand on it, I'm hit with another image of a bat but don't say anything and turn the card over.

Robbie says, "Oh, swords like Jill's."

"You're right. Page of Swords she got. This one is the Knight."

"Pretty badass."

The card depicts a strong man on horseback, weapon at the ready, crows flying overhead. I haven't met a man who didn't like that card. "The knight is bold, courageous, confident. He'll sacrifice anything to achieve his goal."

Before I can warn him about the negative aspects like self-obsession, craftiness, tyranny, he says, "Makes perfect sense."

I place my hand on the card to the left. "This card is past influences that are still affecting you." As I flip it, I'm hit with an image of a shattered mirror. "The Nine of Swords."

"Does it matter if it's upside down?"

"Actually, this one is right side up. The Knight was reversed, but in this deck we can disregard direction."

"So what's this tell you? Doesn't look so good."

"The Nine is sorrow and pain, worry and anxiety, misery and unhappiness."

He's shaking his head like none of those apply. I say, "Could also be trials and tribulations. Something you have to go through to grow."

"I've had my share of those. You wouldn't believe the stuff I've seen at the jail."

"Oh, I'm sure. It could be something even earlier too, maybe childhood." My guardian angel flashes a body lying on a hardwood floor. "Perhaps a death in the family."

Robbie scratches his chin. "Can't think of anyone."

"Alright, we'll move on," I say, not letting it shake my confidence. "The third card signifies the future, what will come of the situation."

"What, no sword?" he says, having fun with it.

"Four of Cups. This is a good one, means you're in for a spiritual awakening."

"Um, not sure how likely that is. I don't even know if I'm capable."

Gently, so he knows it's not an attack, I ask, "Why would you say that?"

There's another thump from below, but he doesn't seem to notice and says, "I'm an atheist. Have been since I was old enough to make up my own mind."

"Spiritual doesn't mean you have to believe in a god, or spirits, or anything like that."

"Okay, as long as I'm not going to start doing yoga and burning incense all day."

I give a little laugh and tap the Four. "You can also think of this as help coming from a powerful source or a different approach to a new problem. New relationship possibilities."

He's smiling, looking right at me. "Well, we might need to check with Jill first."

I tuck my hair behind my ear and pray I'm not blushing. Back to business, I move to the fourth card. "Now, the reasons or causes that led to your situation."

I flip the card which is also reversed. "This is another powerful one. The Moon signifies transition. Emerging talent, psychic powers, solitude, peace."

Robbie stares at the card, his forehead wrinkled. "Umm?"

"Well, it could also reveal obstacles in your way of achieving what you want. It goes with the Nine of Swords and can tell us more about the past event."

"Okay," he says, not looking very impressed.

"Last one." I lay my hand on the card, block the unsettling feeling in my gut. I flip the card and say, "This is what will happen if you stay on your current path."

His smile says he's pleased with the reversed card. "Sweet. I'm going to turn into Gandalf."

I can see why Jill said he was charming. "The Magician. Very powerful male. Creativity, inventiveness, imagination, confidence, wisdom. Although you do have to be careful it doesn't lead to the negative aspects."

"Which are?"

"Well, the Magician is not always a good person and is known for using his power to commit wrongs."

"I'm one of the fairest guards in the jail."

"Perhaps it's not about your job. Do you have power anywhere else? Over anyone?

He shakes his head.

"The important thing to remember is just how these cards all relate to one another."

"So what do they tell you?"

"Well, the overall result could be a couple things depending on your question. If it's—" An even louder thud from below stops me. "Did you hear that?"

"Probably one of the cats."

There's an orange tabby at its water bowl, a fat gray one on the couch. "How many do you have?"

"Two."

There's another thump, this one vibrating through the floor. Goosebumps spread down both arms, my angel bringing back the image of the bat. "Someone's down there."

The house is silent, both of us listening. Robbie says, "Must be a pipe or something."

I get up and walk over to the staircase leading down. I steady my voice and call down, "Who's there?"

No response. I wait for Robbie to call me crazy, but he keeps it to himself and joins my side. He says, "I've actually been hearing noises the last few nights."

My spirit sense is tingling, my body filled with dread. "What's down there?"

"My little mancave. TV and a bar is about it."

I nod down the stairs. "Can we?"

"Of course." He leads the way, but even with all his muscles I'm not so sure he can protect us. There's something down here and it's angry.

We enter the small room, a large TV above the fireplace, a wooden bat on the mantel. I stop in the doorway because, although I can't see anything, there's no ignoring the enraged presence in the middle of the room.

Robbie glances back at me. "You okay? You look like you saw a ghost."

I don't want him thinking I'm nuts, but this is why I was called here, my chance to save a soul. "There's something. It's furious."

He faces the fireplace. "Where?"

I close my eyes and focus on the energy. I reopen them and say, "A foot in front of you. All I see is red. I'd step back."

He does but takes his time to show he's not afraid.

I remember the sage in my glovebox. "I'm going to run to my car. Don't move, just keep repeating these words: Surround me fully and completely. Remove this spirit from my house."

I shout it again as I run up the stairs and out the door, my fight or flight fully kicked in. I grab the sage and lighter from the open glovebox, the pepper spray flying out the door and rolling under the car. The spray won't help so I race back inside and down the stairs, holding my necklace, repeating my mantra. "Protect me."

Robbie's standing right where I left him, not saying a word. A large mirror frame I hadn't noticed before is resting against the wall to his right, the glass removed.

I light the sage and enter the room, my shoes clacking on the hardwood. "Surround me fully and completely. Remove this spirit from my house."

He's looking a bit to the right, where I sense the red blob of energy. He asks, "What is it?"

The energy is lashing out in wide arcs hard enough to disturb the smoke from the sage. "It wants to hurt you. It's attached to you, maybe something from your work."

Without looking at me he says, "Could it be a prisoner?"

I repeat the prayer while making the sign of the cross with the sage. "Maybe. I don't know."

"What should I do?" He sounds nervous now. "Is it saying anything?"

"Say the prayer with me."

Robbie joins the next round then asks, "Is it leaving?"

I make three more crosses, feel the spirit calming. "It's a woman."

Robbie turns to me, his face like stone. "This is crazy."

I'm receiving a message, but it's weak and garbled, maybe nothing more than my imagination. I close my eyes and try to tap into it.

Warn you. Warn you.

"Hold on, I'm getting something." There's a familiar energy I can't place. "She was betrayed."

Robbie backs up to the doorway, his nervousness replaced by anger. "What's that lying bitch telling you?"

The spirit says run, but Robbie's blocking the only exit. An image of a steel pole with a hook at the end comes to me. I don't know what it is, but I understand I'm in danger. "Actually, I was wrong. It's a man. He's saying he used to be your friend."

"Now we got two lying bitches."

My phone's in my purse upstairs, but even if it was in my hand there's no way I could dial 911 before he jumps me. An image of a roaring fire fills my mind.

"This is all your fucking fault," he says, his voice so dark. "Jill wouldn't have gone snooping if it weren't for your reading."

I turn to the fireplace and grab the poker beside it. "Just let me leave. There's nothing here. No one would believe me."

I've got no idea if it's my guardian angel or Jill's spirit, but someone's showing me a homerun, the ball flying out of the park.

Robbie says, "Last chance. Put that down."

Now!

The energy rushes past me and collides with Robbie, the force knocking him back a step, his hands covering his face.

"Nice try, bitch." He lowers his hands, his eyes going wide when he sees me midswing, the poker flying for his face.

The sharp hook of the poker buries deep in his skull, the thud vibrating up my arms. I let it go, but it stays embedded, hanging awkwardly from the side of his head.

Robbie opens his mouth to speak, but nothing comes out.

The ball of energy circles in front of him and knocks him backward, sends him crashing to the floor.

All my strength leaves me as I collapse on the recliner, the image of a cheering crowd dying down until the only thing left is the plop, plop, plop of blood.

Pillow Talk

"This is such a lovely meal. Thanks again for inviting me over," Kerri said as she struggled to scoop up the linguine with her fork.

Phillip looked across the small dining room table set with candles, flowers, and fine china. "I'm just so glad you accepted." He raised his glass of merlot toward her and toasted, "Here's to new beginnings."

The blond blushed the color of the wine and gulped down half her glass. "This is all so new to me. I'm used to dating such jerks. You're the first decent guy I've gone out with. All the others were just overgrown boys."

"This may sound mean, but I'm glad in a way. It's selfish, but if you had found someone special, we would never have met."

Kerri turned toward the dimly lit living room. "You have such a nice, cozy place. It's great."

"Cozy. The translation means small."

"No. No, that's not what I meant at all."

"Relax." Phillip reached across the table and gently stroked her hand. "I was only teasing."

Kerri sighed and placed her free hand on top of Phillip's. "You're sure you're not mad?"

Phillip completed the pile, putting his other hand over hers. "Of course not. I don't upset easily, and even if I did, I could never get angry at such a beautiful woman."

13

Kerri eased back into her chair, leaving his hands on hers. Phillip bet there had been many men that told her she was cute, maybe a handful that said she was pretty, but none had ever told her she was beautiful. But beauty was not the most important characteristic in finding the ideal partner. Kerri had that certain quality he looked for in a woman, and that was what made her so very exceptional.

Kerri broke the silence. "Do you really think I look okay?"

"I do. I really do." Phillip studied her face. "I think you're incredible. I don't want to take anything away from your inner beauty, which is what attracted me to you, but look at yourself. Your eyes are irresistible. Your smile is stunning."

Kerri looked like she was having a hard time believing the compliments, so Phillip toned it down. "And you definitely know how to dress and put yourself together. You don't use too much makeup like most, and you know what colors look good on you. By the way, I meant to tell you that your lipstick is very becoming. What shade of red is it?"

"Springtime Rose."

"Well, it looks great on you. But even without makeup, I'm sure you are just as attractive, if not more. I envy the man that gets to wake up next to your innocent, untouched face."

Kerri removed one of her hands from the pile so she could gulp down more wine. "I don't think you'd want to see me without makeup on."

"I'm not just saying that. I really do."

"Well, if you keep saying those sorts of things, maybe you'll get to."

Phillip stood so he could reach the bottle of wine on the counter and refill their glasses. "Be careful what you say. You're so tempting, I might not be able to help myself."

"And I might not stop you."

Phillip grinned. "Really?"

"We'll see." With an embarrassed smile, she pointed at the paintings on the dining room wall. "In our chats you mentioned you were an artist. Are these yours?"

Phillip understood the girl knew nothing about art, but her question walked a thin line between ignorance and retardation. He shook his head and said, "No, but I wish I had. These are reprints of famous works. This one is Van Gogh's *Starry, Starry Night*. And this one is Picasso's *Old Guitarist*. My favorite, though, is this one. *The Scream* by Edvard Munch.

"I'd love to see some of your paintings. Do you have any of them here?"

"Traditional painting was never my thing. I prefer other mediums than canvas, and my creations are generally too large to put up on such a small wall."

"Like what? What do you paint on?"

"I'm still a bit bashful when it comes to my work. It's not easy to expose yourself like that. Sharing my art is the equivalent of baring my soul."

"Then I'm sure your work is beautiful."

"Maybe I'll show you once we get to know each other better."

"Why not now? Please."

"My masterpiece, the one I've been working on for over a year, is in my bedroom."

"Let's go see it."

"We can't."

"Don't make me beg," she said in a voice that Phillip found more irritating than cute.

"It's not finished yet, and I don't just let anyone into my bedroom."

Kerri licked the wine off her lips. "I'm sure I can convince you to let me in there."

"We'll see," Phillip said, giving her a taste of her own medicine. "If you're done eating, we can go into the living room and relax a bit. We can watch some television if you like."

"Sounds good." Kerri swayed slightly when she got up from the table.

Phillip came to her rescue, wrapping a strong arm around her waist. His grip was supportive and a bit sexual, but she didn't move his hand.

"You okay?" he asked, his voice full of concern.

"Oh yeah. Just a bit tipsy, that's all." They walked toward the living room, each with a glass in hand. "You're trying to get me drunk."

Phillip pulled his arm free, feigning that he was offended. "I wouldn't do a thing like that. I thought you trusted me."

"I do, even though I shouldn't." Kerri took his hand and plopped down onto the black leather loveseat.

Phillip sat down next to her. "Why do you say that?"

"Well, we really don't know much about one another."

"I know your whole life story." Phillip set down his glass and put both of her hands in his. "Twenty-two years old. Associate's degree and working towards your bachelor's. To pay for college, you're working as a waitress. One older sister and two younger brothers. What else should I tell you?"

"You have a good memory, but how do you know those things are true? I could have made it all up."

"You could have, but I knew you weren't lying."

"How could you know that by simply reading my messages?"

"I just had a feeling about you. I could have been lying about myself, too."

"I was afraid of that, especially when you emailed me your picture. I thought you were probably a 400-pound pervert who was going to yank me into the apartment the second I rang the doorbell."

Phillip swirled his wine. "So you're okay with the way I look?"

"Are you kidding? You're great." Her hand caressed his forearm. "Very handsome and you look so strong."

"That's just the wine talking."

Kerri downed the rest of her glass. "It does loosen me up, helps me say the things I'd normally never reveal."

"That's good to know."

Kerri leaned over and placed a gentle kiss on his cheek. "I'm so glad I decided to come over. You have no idea what a fresh and wonderful change you are."

"Don't say that yet. You haven't seen all my flaws. I've only let you see my strong points. That's rule number one in the dating handbook. But I do understand why you said you were hesitant to come over. If I was a female, I wouldn't go alone to a stranger's. Hell, to tell you the truth, I was a little nervous having you come over here. It takes a lot of trust to meet like this."

"Well, Mom always said if I let fear run my life, I'd never experience anything, the good along with the bad."

"That's great advice and I'm glad you live by it." He pointed at her glass. "Care for a refill?"

"I do, but I shouldn't. I'm already a little drunk and I have to drive home."

"You don't have to."

"You wouldn't mind if I stayed?"

"Of course not. You can sleep in the bed and I'll crash on the couch like a true gentleman."

Kerri set her glass down and rested her hand on his thigh. "What if I don't want you to be a gentleman?"

"Well, I guess I don't have to."

"What if I want you to kiss me?"

"Then I guess I'll have to oblige," he said, leaning in and pecking her on the cheek.

"Too gentlemanly. I need more than that."

Phillip held the back of her head and placed three very slow and sensual kisses down the length of her neck.

"Much better," she whispered, "but what about my lips?"

He slid further down her neck. "I don't want to mess up your lipstick."

"I can always fix it later."

Phillip rose and nibbled on her lips, finally parting them with his tongue. Kerri moaned and pulled him in closer. Without a word they headed for the bedroom.

Phillip stopped outside his door. "Okay, you fix your makeup in the bathroom and meet me in here. I have to make some preparations."

Kerri closed the bathroom door behind her and Phillip slipped into his room. Fortunately, he had planned ahead in case things worked out between them. He wanted everything to be perfect for her.

Phillip finished his preparations and lay on his king-size bed. Kerri stood awe-struck in the doorway taking in the dozens of scented candles and scattered roses marking her path.

Phillip waved her over, cautioning her to watch her step. He could only imagine what would happen if she kicked over a candle and set fire to his place.

The candlelight flickered over her face when she crawled onto the bed. He was happy to see that she had used her time wisely in the bathroom. Unlike some men, Phillip cared what his lover looked like. He wanted to see every detail of her face as they became intimate so that after she was gone he would be able to remember exactly what she looked like.

Phillip stared into Kerri's eyes and gave her a gentle kiss on her cheek. "You look beautiful."

"Thank you," she said, a little out of breath. "So do you trust me enough to show me your masterpiece?"

"Of course. Lie on your back and look up."

Her mouth gaped as she took in his biggest and best creation, which covered nearly 80 square feet of the ceiling, over twice the size of the bed. It wasn't perfect, but it was close.

"Oh my God, Phillip. It's beautiful."

He pointed at the three patches of exposed ceiling, each measuring two square feet. "It's not finished yet."

Her hand glided across Phillip's chest and stomach. "What kind of material is it?"

"Guess."

"It's kinda hard to tell in this light but it looks like a sheet that you stapled in a bunch of different spots. It's cool how the material droops a little everywhere the splotches of paint are."

"Very observant, but it's not paint and not quite a sheet. You're very close though."

She played with his belt buckle, not sounding very interested when she asked, "So how'd you decide the colors?"

Phillip rolled on top of her so he straddled her waist. "It might sound strange, but I feel fate chose them for me."

The belt pulled free, and her pudgy fingers unbuttoned his pants. "So when are you going to finish the last pieces?"

Phillip touched her lips and Kerri sucked on his finger, teased the tip with her tongue. He pulled it out and ran it across her lips again and then looked down at his fingertip. "I'll do one piece tonight and the other two before the month is over."

"I want to see it before you put it up."

"I'm afraid you won't be able to."

"Why not?" she pouted. "I thought I could stay the whole night."

"Oh, you will. It's just that you're going to help me create it."

Phillip grabbed the pillow beside him and covered the confused look on Kerri's face, pinning the thick pillow down on either side of her head. She flailed her arms and tried to buck him off, but he wouldn't budge.

Kerri whipped her head from side to side and clawed at Phillip's arms, her nails biting deeply into his sweater but only grazing his skin, causing him to laugh.

Soon her movements slowed, then ceased completely. Phillip waited a full minute, ignoring his twitching triceps and burning forearms, before removing the pillow.

Kerri's lifeless face, frozen in fear, a perfect picture of terror, didn't really interest Phillip. Although he did take pleasure in the murder, his main interest was the art. Carefully, he turned the pillow over and slipped off its white case. He held it out before him and admired the work created by Kerri's death throes. Thick lines of Springtime Rose intertwined with the faint circles of reddish blush. Black mascara smudges combined with the hint of light blue eyeshadow. All the colors mixing and blending into a unique piece that held so much meaning and marked yet another climactic chapter in Phillip's creation.

Phillip meticulously tacked the pillowcase to a section of exposed ceiling. Now he wasn't so sure he could finish telling the tale in just two more chapters. In fact, he thought that he'd have to find an apartment with a much larger bedroom. And he was going to have to find it soon.

Results Guaranteed

The chemistry lab was empty, Friday classes cancelled thanks to the memorial service for Ted and the rest of the guys. Peter locked the door, set the half-empty energy drink on his desk, and powered up his outdated computer, which was nothing like the new models they had in the athletic department.

Peter kept his desk spotless, everything in its place, all the angles nice and even. The only thing off this morning was the yellow sticky note resting on his mousepad. Taped to the middle of the paper was a small sewing pin with the professor's chicken scratch circled around it. *The pin is mightier than the sword.*

The professor left weekly challenges for Peter and Suki as a fun way to get his research assistants thinking outside the box. But with two dozen dead students about to be buried, trying to figure out a word puzzle was a hundred rungs down Peter's ladder. Still, Peter's mind couldn't help playing with the words, rearranging them, wondering what the circle meant.

He set his brown leather messenger bag on top of the note - out of sight, out of mind. With no need to check emails, Peter inserted his flash drive and opened the Hex80 file. He knew the protocol by heart, but scanning the document lifted his spirits. What had started as a disappointing insecticide now had incredible potential, largely because of the unconventional thinking the professor encouraged. Any scientist would say the results were amazing, but Peter understood they had to be duplicated before he could shop for a buyer.

The front section of his upper desk drawer was lined with blue, black, and red pens, with two silver sharpies at the edge. At the back was the box of chemical-resistant rubber gloves, size small because Peter hadn't grown much since junior high.

Peter slipped on his lab coat, goggles, then the gloves, took a dozen flyers and a nylon rope from his bag. After one last look at the screen, he downed the rest of the Blast Off and tossed it in the trashcan. "Here we go."

The safety shower took up the far corner of the lab. Peter pulled up a metal stand outside the shower and set the papers on it, strung the rope back and forth across the top of the shower several times.

All the supplies were under the counter against the side wall. He filled a tray with 2000 milliliters of solvent and added the exact amount of each chemical, no need to alter a winning combination.

Careful not to spill, Peter brought the tray to the stand with the flyers on it, 12 two-inch-long slits cut into the bottom of each piece. He took the first flyer and lowered it in the solution, held it under for a ten-count before pinning it to the makeshift clothesline, repeating the process 11 more times.

Peter peeled off his gloves and tossed them into the chemical waste container, dried his fingers on a paper towel. Usually his hands didn't sweat so much, but he chalked it up to nervousness; so much was riding on this product.

The flyers needed 15 minutes for the last traces of solvent to evaporate. Peter took off his coat and goggles, returned to his computer and searched for the latest on the deaths. The police still had no clue how a quarter of the university's football team, as well as three other students, mysteriously died during the 18-hour period between Tuesday night and Wednesday afternoon.

There were no signs of foul play, but the police were investigating the possibility of poisoning, maybe a certain type of nutritional supplement. When it was pointed out that three nonplayers also died, police responded that all three were well-built, athletic young men who perhaps used the same unknown product. They wouldn't know for sure until the toxicology reports were back on Monday.

Peter closed the article, confident the tests would show absolutely nothing. No poisoned protein bars would be found in their intestines. They wouldn't find the slightest traces of any foreign chemicals. Everything would appear normal.

What did come as a surprise to Peter was that the police had failed to come up with any clues. He hadn't expected the campus police to make the connection, but the state investigators should have by now. Thorough searches should have revealed each stiff had a small slip of ripped paper with a telephone number on it. The kind of slip that people tore off the bottom of flyers; slips that promised things too good to be true, like gaining ten pounds of muscle in two weeks.

Peter wiped his forehead, jumped in his seat when the door clicked and pushed open. "Professor Garvel. What are you doing here?"

Gray-haired Garvel looked so different in jeans and a t-shirt. He closed the door and said, "I got an alert that someone was in the lab. I thought you and Suki would be at the service."

Peter hadn't realized the lab was monitored but wasn't concerned. "Thought I'd get in some extra work."

Garvel checked his watch. "You are attending it, aren't you? You can make it if you hurry."

Peter prayed Garvel didn't look to his left. Hoping the professor would leave if Peter got emotional, he shook his head. Trying to sound sad, he said, "I just can't. I've always struggled with death."

Garvel walked over, set his hand on Peter's shoulder, his first ever display of affection. "Isn't your roommate one of the deceased?"

"Yeah, afraid so." Peter turned off his screen and wiped his forehead, wished he'd turned on the AC. "Ted. Great guy."

Garvel said, "I'm so sorry." He gave Peter's shoulder a squeeze and sat down at Suki's desk, swiveled the chair so it faced Peter. "I'm all ears if you care to talk."

Figuring Garvel had dealt with his own bullies, Peter said, "He wasn't like the other jocks. It's a shame he had to die."

"The whole thing is just awful." Garvel studied Peter and said, "You sure you don't want to go? I can clean up in here."

"Tell you the truth, I'm not feeling so good. And honestly, half the school is going to be there. No one's going to miss me."

"You don't look good. Did you go out last night?"

Peter had a difficult time swallowing his spit. "I don't drink."

Garvel nodded and got up, walked straight for the safety shower. "So what are you working on? Is this the Hexycar—"

"Don't touch them!"

The professor pulled back his hand like it'd been slapped, looked at Peter for an explanation.

"I'm sorry. I just can't mess those up."

Garvel turned back to the shower, stepped to the side so he could read the big print at the top of each flyer. "Results Guaranteed."

Peter tried to stand then thought better of it, afraid he might faint. He shouldn't have had the energy drink on an empty stomach.

The professor returned to Suki's chair. "Hope those flyers aren't for something you're selling."

Peter wanted to say no but found it difficult to speak and simply shook his head.

"That's good. A claim like that would be sure to bring lawsuits, not to mention the FDA pounding down your door."

A shiver ripped through Peter. He tried to cover it by hugging himself and asking, "You cold?"

Garvel shook his head. Staring in Peter's saucer-sized eyes, he said, "No. Not like you."

"I should go."

"By all means," Garvel said, motioning toward the door. "What should I do with your flyers?"

Peter swallowed a mouthful of spit, his throat making him wince. "I'll get them."

"Twelve's a lot. You really need that many?"

"For a friend." Peter pulled the flash drive and put it in his bag, his fingers and forearms slick with sweat.

"The info's still on there," Garvel said, pointing at the computer. "I'm guessing you forgot all sessions are recorded. Remember, your work is owned by the university."

Fuck. That was one calculation Peter had screwed up. He rubbed his eyes but when he opened them, the Professor was back at the shower.

Garvel moved his finger as he counted. "Twelve slips at the bottom of each flyer. 144." Garvel nodded and almost to himself said, "Make senses you'd want a square."

Peter closed and opened his eyes again, disappointed it didn't fix his vision. Everything was blurry, the outer edges too bright. "It's a friend's."

Garvel mumbled as he read the page. He smiled when he finished. "Well done, Peter. At least this time you didn't have to lie."

"I feel really sick," Peter said, laying his head on the desk.

"Lose unwanted weight fast. Results guaranteed." Garvel sat down on the corner of Peter's desk. Sounding like he really wanted to know, he said, "I get why you hated the jocks, but what have you got against fat people?"

A dull thrum picked up speed in the back of Peter's head. "Help."

"First you've got to tell me if you figured out today's challenge."

The messenger bag fell to the ground as Peter fumbled for the sticky piece of paper. He shrieked when the sewing pin pierced his palm. Holding the note an inch from his face, he said, "My fingers were wet."

"Good, good," Garvel said, cheering on his student. "Now you're thinking."

Peter threw open his drawer, pulled out the box of gloves. Tears ran down his cheeks, his fingers trembling as they examined the gloves for pinpricks. "Why?"

"The dictators I'll be offering your formula to will feel safer if I don't have a partner. Plus, it's going to make me a fortune and I'd rather not share."

The Hole

It was nine in the evening when we got the keys to our new home. I was exhausted from sparring and we weren't moving in for another month, but Hailey said she just had to see it.

Hailey ran around the first floor and bounded up the staircase, calling for me to follow. I nearly told her I was too tired and that she should hurry up, but her beautiful brown eyes were shimmering with excitement.

After verifying the upstairs rooms were exactly as they'd been at the final walk-through five days before, I persuaded her to go downstairs. I was halfway out the door when Hailey opened the closet and peered inside.

"Tony, what's that hole doing there?"

I tried to hide my impatience; I'd mentioned the hole to her during the walk-through. "Don't worry about it."

Hailey pouted. "You're mad at me."

"No, just hungry and tired."

She closed the closet and said, "Sorry, it just doesn't look like it should be there. Do you know what it's for?"

I had no idea why the jagged-edged two-foot-by-two-foot hole was carved into the back wall of the closet. I figured the previous owner must have done it because it didn't look like the work of a professional. It was more like the handiwork of a drunken, chainsaw-wielding midget or an animal that clawed its way through.

Hailey thought I knew everything about everything, but I didn't know the first thing concerning a house. Electrical. Mechanical. All that stuff was foreign to me. I knew how to knock people out and how to break things, not fix them.

Knowing that I shouldn't, I matter of factly told her, "The agent said that's how the blood-thirsty beast that lives under the house gets out."

Hailey slapped my shoulder. "Why'd you say that?" she whined. "I'm never going to sleep here by myself. You're such a jerk sometimes."

"Relax, babe, I was just joking around."

"Well it's not funny."

"Yeah it is. Look, there is no monster living under the house. It was obviously a joke."

"Don't patronize me. I'm not a child."

"Then think like an adult," I said, my impatience getting the best of me. "There's nothing to be afraid of."

"I know, but you shouldn't have said that. Last time you scared me I almost wet myself."

I laughed but stopped when she teared up. I hugged her and said, "I really am sorry, babe. I'll cover up the hole and you'll never have to worry about it again."

Hailey settled down. "I don't like being by myself, especially in a big house like this. Plus, you're always out of town for your fights." She wiped a bead of perspiration off my forehead. "Why are you sweating so much?"

"It's too damn hot in here. I set the AC for 68 degrees, but haven't felt anything coming out of the vents. Remind me to call about it if it's not working tomorrow."

"And yet another expense."

"Nah, the home warranty will cover it. Are you ready to go? I'll turn off the lights," I said, moving toward the kitchen before she objected.

I was turning off the kitchen lights when the front door opened and closed. A noise came from the other room. I crept toward the hallway knowing it had to be Hailey hoping to scare me. I paused at the refrigerator when a muffled shuffle came from around the corner. I leapt into the hallway and yelled.

No one was there. The hallway was empty.

I felt foolish standing there with my arms above my head like an enraged bear. I was extra sensitive to the verbal slipups, tongue-twisters, and slurred speech I'd been experiencing, and didn't want to even consider I might have imagined it. That's probably why it was so easy for me to write it off as being a new-house noise that I had to adjust to.

***

We moved into the house four weeks later with our motley crew of fur babies: Duke, our 13-year-old, deaf and dying golden retriever; Rollo, our obscenely obese cat; and his skinny sister, Hoppity, who was missing her right rear leg. Tired from a long day of moving, but wanting to start off our life in the house right, I turned off the lights and carried Hailey up the stairs and laid her on the bed.

I thought Hailey was going to kiss me, but out of nowhere she asked, "You covered up that hole, right?"

"What hole?"

"The one in the downstairs closet." When I hesitated, she said, "Tony, you promised."

"It'll be fine."

Hailey sat up. "What does that mean? Did you cover it or not?"

I rolled over and turned my back to her. "What it means is I'm really freaking tired and it doesn't need to be covered right now."

"You promised."

I got out of bed. "Why can't you just let it go? Is it too much to ask to enjoy the night?"

"Forget it then. Do it tomorrow."

I mumbled, "No. I promised. I'm up now anyway." I left the room and stood in the dark hallway. I couldn't find the light switch and yelled, "Where's the goddamn flashlight?"

"Next to the fridge," she snapped.

I headed down the stairs, one hand on the handrail, the other dragging against the wall. At the bottom I reached out for the light switch on the wall in front of me. A loud, piercing shriek sliced through the silence. I jerked my foot back and fell to the floor.

I grabbed my right wrist that was already throbbing. "Goddamn cat."

The bedroom light flashed on and Hailey appeared in the doorway. "What happened? Are you okay?"

I got up and headed for the kitchen to get an ice pack. "I'd better be. That could've been my career."

The next day Hailey worked at the animal hospital until seven, and I spent time at the physical therapist's rehabilitating my wrist and doing some light conditioning. When she got home, I turned up the television. I didn't want her asking about the hole which I'd only covered with a piece of cardboard.

31

Neither one of us said a word until after dinner when Hailey asked, "Mind if I turn the air back on?"

"It's on."

"Care if I turn the thermostat down then? It's hot in here."

I was in the recliner, wearing nothing but my boxers and wrist brace. "I feel fine."

"I didn't ask how you felt." Hailey stormed up the stairs. She returned a minute later and stood in front of the television. "Having it set at 85 isn't exactly what I would describe as 'having the air on.'"

"I set it at 76 before I left for rehab. Are you sure you read it right?"

"It's digital."

"I guess I didn't set it for 76," I said, hoping she would believe my lie. I was positive I had.

***

Saturdays were usually spent sparring, but since I couldn't train, I told Hailey I was hers for the day. We did lunch at Hailey's favorite restaurant, took in a chick flick, got her a new purse, and finished it with dinner at In 'N' Out.

When we got home it was time to feed the kids. The second the can opener started to buzz, Hoppity came sliding in, rubbing against Hailey's calves, meowing for her to hurry. Rollo, however, was nowhere to be seen.

The 20-pound cat never missed a meal. Hailey dished the food onto a paper plate and I scouted the house, calling for Fat Cat. He wasn't downstairs, wasn't in the guest room, the office or the bedroom.

I changed into boxers and headed back for the stairs. When I passed the thermostat, the air conditioner was turned off and the temperature was 84 degrees. I switched it back on and set it for 68.

I joined Hailey, who was relaxing on the couch, and asked her, "Did Rollo come out?"

"Nope. He wasn't upstairs?"

"I didn't see him. Maybe he's in the garage."

"I doubt it. I don't think he could make it through that kitty door."

We both laughed at the thought of our obese cat sticking halfway through the swinging door. I asked, "By the way, did you happen to turn off the air before we left?"

"No. Wasn't it on?"

I shook my head. "I'm going to call that repair guy out here again. That's two days in a row the thing's screwed up."

"What do you think is wrong with it?"

I had no idea, but I was a macho idiot that didn't want my wife to know that. Before realizing what a mistake I was making, I blurted out, "Maybe the little monster under the house prefers the heat."

"Damn it, Tony!" She leapt off the coach and headed upstairs. "I told you not to say stuff like that."

That night, I had trouble sleeping because of the pain in my wrist. I woke around two to a noise downstairs. I listened carefully but all I could hear was Hoppity, who was curled up against my head, purring loudly. I placed her by my feet and recognized the familiar sound of nails tapping on the tiled floor below.

I was drifting back to sleep when a terrifying thought got me out bed. It hadn't been Duke downstairs. He had to stay upstairs with us, locked in the master bathroom by a baby-gate because of his bladder problem. The gate was still up and Duke was spread out on the shower floor.

At the doorway I peered into the darkness, straining to hear anything out of the ordinary. There was complete silence, not even the air conditioner blasting air through the vents.

I flipped on the hallway lights and checked the thermostat. The temperature setting had somehow leapt from 65 to 85, but the current temperature was 67. The settings had changed in the past couple of minutes, right about the time I had heard the noise.

After resetting the thermostat to seventy degrees, I forced myself to check the house, a two-hundred-pound professional athlete spooked by a strange noise and screwy central air system.

I'd seen clips of cats and dogs turning doorknobs, hitting light switches, and even flipping on televisions. Rollo had slept on the table the day we moved in. It wasn't difficult to picture him stretching up and placing a paw on one of the touch pads that adjusted the temperature. But to turn off the AC, Rollo would have had to pull the lower part of the casing down and then push the switch to the right. Not even the most talented cat in the world could pull that off.

I understood that the switch had to be manipulated by someone or something. I picked up the table beneath it and set it in the office before going back to bed.

When I woke the next morning, Hailey was already at church. I ate my breakfast downstairs and noticed the house was uncomfortably warm. I set my half-eaten bowl of oatmeal on top of the refrigerator so the cats wouldn't get into it and headed upstairs.

The air conditioner was off and the current temperature was 84 degrees, the table back underneath. Hailey must not have cared for my redecorating.

I set the air for 70 and went down to finish breakfast. With nothing else to do, I went into the garage and gathered a few small pieces of plywood, a hammer, and some nails. I hated my hesitation standing outside the closet.

I stepped inside the closet and found myself standing on the piece of cardboard I had covered the hole with. The suction from the door opening must have pulled the cardboard from the wall.

There was still no sign of Rollo, so I got a can of cat food, peeled back the lid and called for him. Confident he wasn't in the walls of the house, I banged the nails into the plywood.

Twenty minutes later, Hailey came home, the scowl on her face telling me that the sermon was not about forgiveness.

From my spot on the couch, I asked, "How was church?"

She set her purse on the dining room table and didn't say a word.

"Look, I'm really sorry about last night. Can't we just forget about that?"

"No, we can't just forget about it. Don't you see? I can't forget about it. Why do you think I tell you not to joke about those sorts of things? It's because I can't get the thoughts out of my head once they're in there. Do you know what I dreamt about all last night? I'll give you one guess."

"I'm sorry."

"All I could think about was this tiny little demon that lives under the house and comes out at night when we sleep. I know it's silly and irrational, but I could barely sleep, and now I feel lousy."

"I didn't mean for that to happen. This is our first home and we're supposed to be enjoying it. And you shouldn't feel stupid for thinking about my joke. I've freaked myself out, too."

She shook her head. "You scared yourself?"

"Sort of. A little, I guess. Don't tell my friends," I said with a smile. "I even nailed the hole up while you were gone."

"That's nice to know, but you were supposed to have done that a couple of days ago."

"By the way, did you happen to move that table under the thermostat this morning?"

Hailey gave me a strange look. "From where?"

"You didn't touch it?"

Hailey walked into the kitchen. "No. Why? Is something wrong with it?" She shouted, "Maybe our little friend under the house moved it."

I didn't detect any malice in her voice, but I wished I could have seen her face. At first I thought she was trying to make peace and show me she could take a joke, but then everything started to make sense. Hailey had been paying me back since the day we moved in, playing a sick practical joke on me. She was changing the thermostat's settings to get me worked up and now moving the table to really get me going.

I felt like a fool for covering up the hole and admitting I was freaked out. I waited for her to come back and laugh at me, but she didn't. Maybe she was planning on taking it further and making me look even more stupid. I didn't care because I would be ready for it.

That night, I slept incredibly well. Except for the dream with clicking on the floor downstairs, it was the best sleep I had had all week.

After Hailey left for work in the morning, I checked the closet. At first glance, everything looked normal except the plywood looked loose. The top corners of the board pulled right out from the wall like someone had removed it and then carefully put it back in. I pushed the board back against the wall, thinking either I had seriously underestimated Hailey's practical joking skills or I was going completely insane.

That night in my sparring session, I took a tremendous left hook to my temple that put me on the canvas, my third concussion in a month. Even after resting at the gym for an hour, the intense pounding in my head made it hard for me to think, and I had a difficult time driving home. Hailey saw I was in serious pain and helped me up the stairs and into bed where I quickly fell asleep.

A loud thud woke me from my sleep at three. I asked Hailey if she'd heard something, but she didn't answer. I reached out for her, but she wasn't there. I sat up, ignoring my pounding head and looked around the room. Duke lay in the shower, and Hoppity was curled between my legs, but Hailey was nowhere to be seen.

I rolled over to Hailey's side and pulled out the 12-inch designer knife from under the mattress. Something scampered down the stairs. I rushed into the hallway, hurried down the stairs in time to see something at the bottom turn the corner toward the kitchen. It was too dark to make out, but it looked too big to be Rollo.

My head thudded like it was ready to crack, but I didn't let it slow me down. A door slammed shut. A second later, I flipped on the downstairs hallway light and ripped open the closet door.

The closet was empty, the loose plywood lying on the floor. Maybe Hailey had placed it like that on purpose, but even if she had, what did I see running down the stairs? I heard it, too. It couldn't be a hallucination brought on by the head trauma. It was real.

My head hurt so bad I could barely stand. I backed out of there and sat in the hallway, propped against the door. I set the knife down and called Hailey's name.

No response, the entire house silent. I wanted to get up and look for her, but I couldn't move. Part of me was too afraid to leave the door unguarded, and the other part thought Hailey could be hiding nearby, waiting to jump out and laugh at my cowardice.

The rumble of the garage door got me to my feet, amplifying the pressure in my head. I staggered into the garage and wiped the tears from my eyes.

Hailey stepped out of her Nissan. She was in her work scrubs which didn't make much sense considering the time. I asked, "Where were you? I was worried sick."

"Dr. Lawson called at one for an emergency c-section. You didn't hear the phone, and I didn't want to wake you, so I left a note on your nightstand."

We headed inside where I wiggled in front of Hailey to block her view of the knife on the ground. Hailey headed upstairs, pausing at the top. She continued towards the bedroom and said, "I hope you plan on cleaning that up in the morning."

I trudged upstairs and saw that the potted plant that normally sat on the table beneath the thermostat lay shattered on the ground, dirt scattered all over the carpet. *The thud that woke me.*

I scooped up as much dirt as possible, then got into bed with Hailey and listened to her play-by-play of the Doberman's surgery. I finally broke away by saying I was thirsty and wanted to get a glass of water.

Being thirsty was a lie, but I needed to retrieve the knife; it was proof of how scared I was when she was gone. She'd love that one.

When I got downstairs the knife wasn't in front of the closet. It hadn't been kicked into the kitchen. It was nowhere to be seen, and Hailey hadn't left my sight since she came home.

Combined with the headache, it was all too much to handle. I went upstairs and made sure Duke and Hoppity were both in the bedroom. As quietly as I could, I locked the door and climbed into bed.

When I woke at ten o'clock, my headache wasn't as severe, but it still hurt. I rolled over to ask Hailey for some aspirin, but she wasn't in the bed or the room.

There was something on her nightstand though. The knife.

Hailey must have found it. I went downstairs to ask her and found a note stating she was at work.

I called her work and got only coldness when she asked, "What do you want?"

"I was just calling to see what time you were coming home. I was surprised you had to go in so early."

"Look, Tony, I'm really busy and can't talk right now. I'll be home by five." She hung up before I had a chance to ask her about the knife.

I considered calling her back but figured I'd better not. Besides, she must have put it back. One of the animals had probably pushed the knife into the kitchen and Hailey had found it. I'd had enough of the hole, even if it was just my imagination. It was time to seal it up for good. I locked Hoppity and Duke in the bedroom, then went into the closet to check one last time for Rollo, who had now been missing for nearly three days.

It was hard to see anything, but the flashlight reflected off something in the far corner. I thought it resembled the small bell from Rollo's collar, but the eye strain brought back my headache and blurred my vision. After calling one last time for Rollo, I bricked up the hole and nailed a bed sheet over it to cover my less-than-perfect work. Hailey would question why I resorted to such an extreme measure, and the last thing I needed was for her to complain about its appearance.

Finally, I installed a sturdy padlock to ensure the door couldn't be opened from the inside or outside without the key. Hailey wouldn't like the looks of the new addition, but I'd worry about that later.

I walked around the outside of the house, searching for vents or openings to the crawl space beneath the house. There weren't any in the backyard, so I headed to the front and heard my name being called.

My neighbor across the street waved. I walked over and shook his hand. "How are you doing, sir?"

"I'm great. You are Tony "The Destroyer" Demonte, aren't you?"

I was just on the verge of becoming famous, and it was still a surprise when people recognized me. I said, "Guilty as charged."

"It's a pleasure to meet you. I just saw you tear apart Johnson in May. Let me tell you, you're gonna be one hell of a boxer."

"Thank you, Mr. …"

"Oh, it's Warner, but please call me Jack."

"Well, Jack, it's nice meeting you. You're the first neighbor I've met since we moved in."

Jack's smile faded. "You live there?"

"Yeah. My wife and I bought it about a month ago, but we just moved in this week. We got a great deal on the place."

"So…" Jack hesitated, "how do you guys like living there?"

"To tell you the truth, I really don't care for it all that much. I like the neighborhood, but not the house."

Jack seemed uneasy. He said, "It's getting pretty hot out here. Why don't you come on in and have something cold to drink? We can talk more."

I followed him into his house. When I walked out an hour later, I was quite shaken up. I wondered if it was it possible Hailey had convinced this nice old man to get in on the practical joke and help scare me.

Despite having strong reservations, Jack told me about the bad luck that had plagued the four families who had lived there in the past five years. I listened to the stories of runaway pets, abducted children, and spouses that picked up and left without notice, in such a hurry they left all their belongings behind.

One or two of the stories happening would have been understandable, but how could so much misfortune happen in one place? I didn't believe in the supernatural, but I did believe in statistics. Something was wrong with that house, and we were moving out of it, regardless of the financial loss. Maybe we'd even be able to sue the broker for keeping the house's history from us.

My real estate agent's number was on the fridge. I grabbed my cell and was about to call her when I noticed the missed call and voice mail notification.

I wiped the sweat off my forehead and retrieved the message. It was Hailey.

"Hi, honey. Just calling to say sorry about earlier. I didn't mean to be so rude; I'm just tired. Promise I'll make it up to you later. I'm taking off now, so I'll see you in 20 minutes. Love you, babe."

The time stamp revealed that she'd called just minutes after I had stepped outside. I ran to the garage and saw Hailey's car.

She wasn't on the lower level, so I headed upstairs. I glanced at the thermostat that was set for 90 degrees – the highest setting.

I sprinted downstairs and tried to pull open the closet, forgetting I had locked it. I pulled the padlock key from my pocket and fumbled with the lock, ripped the bed sheet off the wall. Everything was exactly as I had left it.

Maybe Hailey had gone for a walk or was tanning in the backyard. She'd barely left the house except to work or shop, but neither had I before today. Maybe this was part of her joke.

I splashed water on my face in the bathroom and peered into the mirror, unsurprised that I looked as awful as I felt. If I was going mad, would I be sane enough to realize it?

Something caught my eye in the lower corner of the mirror. I spun around and collapsed to the floor in front of the dark hole that had been freshly carved into the wall.

***

My lawyer said that when the police found me, I was balled up on the bathroom floor, wailing like a newborn baby. The drops of Hailey's blood on the floor and the bloodstains that they formed on my jeans weren't enough to convict me of my wife's murder. Her bare bones, which they found neatly piled behind the brick wall I had built, were however.

A lot of people say I should have gotten the death penalty. I agree with them. That would have been the humane thing to do, but they won't give me the injection because of my mental state. That evil little bastard got me good. Not only did it kill my wife, it pinned it on me and made it so I have to replay it over and over again for the rest of my life in this nuthouse.

No One's Home

No One lived in this apartment over 30 years ago. This is the bedroom I shared with Mother when she wasn't working.

It was a different bed then, nowhere near as comfy and nice. This one is soft, the black silk sheet so slippery. Mother's sheets were all different colors, piled in the corner until I'd take them downstairs to the laundry, my hands getting gross and sticky.

No One rarely slept in Mother's bed because she worked every night she wasn't bleeding. There was a pillow in the closet where I curled up when I tired of her show.

The closet door no longer has slats to peek through; the walls are painted a pretty blue. The room smells of roses and happiness instead of semen and sadness.

Lot's of times, I'd silently cry myself to sleep, but not tonight. No One couldn't be happier to be back. No One likes to remember, to see how things have changed.

The rest of this city is just as dirty as it's ever been, but this apartment's found new life, a young couple giving it their best shot. Instead of our scratchy brown rug covering the faded floorboards, there's a thick dark carpet that hides any sign I was here.

Seventeen sets of renters have lived here in the last three decades, but none of them knew how much of Mother's blood was soaked up by the wood they walked on. She'd been sitting right there, combing her hair for her next visitor, no warning before my knife slit her throat.

I slide off the bed and slip on Marty's sandals. At first it felt strange to be stepping into another man's shoes, but after what we've shared, it only seems right. Marty's the good-looking guy cuddled next to Maggie in the photo on the dresser, *Maggie and Marty Forever* etched into the wooden frame.

On the door to Mother's rough-up room there's a huge poster of Maggie with her winning smile, a big thumbs up in front of a for sale sign, her phone number blue and bold on the bottom. Her office is tiny but clean, everything organized, nothing like the whips and chains, masks and gags Mother laid out on her work bench. It cost extra to go in that room, Mother always coming out limping, a new bruise or black eye as part of her bonus.

The living room is just as small as I remember; their over-sized couch and wide-screen TV filling up the space. No One was rarely allowed in this room though because this is where men waited while Mother cleaned up or finished off a friend.

The parking spot is only ten feet from the front door, and it's easy to hear the car pull in and shut off, a door open then close. I ease into the kitchen, careful not to slip on the slick tiles. I press my back to the wall and slide out my knife, smile when Marty opens the door, calls for Maggie.

He closes the door, turns the lock. "Maggie, you here? Hey, hun, you in the kitchen?"

No One stays silent as his footsteps come closer. No One knows what's going to happen, how he'll freeze when he sees what a mess I made out of Maggie, pieces of her scattered across the floor.

Sorry, Marty. No One's home.

News First

One hundred yards south of the library's entrance, hiding safely behind a large brick dormitory, Nick trained his camera on the woman he'd had a crush on for the past year.

"Good afternoon. This is Amanda Harrington with Channel Six news. We are first on the grisly scene here in Providence, Rhode Island, on typically tranquil College Hill.

"Ghastly images of the Virginia Tech massacre flash through my mind as I try to comprehend what I'm seeing. Reminiscent of the 1966 University of Texas tower shooting, a madman barricaded himself on top of Brown University's 16-story Sciences Library and started firing indiscriminately on the innocent below. In the last five minutes he has killed 17 and wounded well over two dozen."

Amanda did a little shake of her head, tossing her long blond hair over her shoulder. "Police are trying desperately to cordon off and evacuate a six-block radius around the library, which stands at the corner of Thayer and Waterman streets. They are seriously undermanned for such a large endeavor and are anxiously awaiting reinforcements from state troopers.

"Stay clear of this area at all costs. Those of you in the area should evacuate if you can do so. If not, find shelter in your basements. The gunman is on one of the tallest buildings in the city and has a tremendous view. Reports indicate that he has launched at least one grenade along with his barrage of bullets. Stay tuned, we'll be right back as soon as we get an update."

Nick lowered his camera and flashed a smile. The shapely reporter with the sculpted cheekbones, smooth skin, and luscious lips was even more beautiful than she was behind the viewfinder. "That was great."

Amanda pulled a small compact out of her jacket and flipped it open. "It was, wasn't it?"

"We lucked out on this one. I was dreading doing that story on the football team, but it looks like it turned out for the best."

"Damn right it did. Know what this means? We're talking at least one journalism award. This is my ticket to the big time. I'll be seen all around the nation tonight. They'll be showing me on every station, and before you know it I'll finally be out of this crappy state."

"You'll be taking me with you, right?"

"We'll see. Can't promise you anything." She checked her phone. "Any word on who this nutcase is? Have the choppers gotten a look at him yet?"

"They won't send in our helicopter team while he's still up there shooting."

Thick lines creased her forehead. "Those spineless bastards. We need footage of this guy. Video of me standing in front of a brick wall won't cut it."

"But the police won't even fly in yet."

"Then they're even worse. They get paid to put their life on the line."

Gunshots shattered the silence. Nick and Amanda threw themselves against the wall even though they were out of harm's way. When the ten-second hailstorm of bullets stopped, Nick straightened up and snuck a peak around the corner.

"That dude's got some heavy duty equipment up there. That wasn't your average rifle."

Amanda dusted off her short skirt. "Well, what is it? I need details."

"I don't know. Some kind of machine gun I guess."

Amanda pulled out her phone and called their boss, Jonathan. "Send in the chopper," she said. "I need footage now. No other channels are here yet, but they will be soon."

Although Amanda was incredibly beautiful, Nick also admired her intensity and dedication to her job. All their co-workers labeled her the Ice Queen, but if she had been a man they'd only have praise for her.

"I don't care," she said into the phone. "Then get a camera man on the roof of one of the surrounding buildings."

Putting a co-worker in the line of fire, however, was going past dedication. Nick considered telling her that, but judging by the disgusted look on her face, Jonathan just had.

"Give me something to go back on the air with. What's he shooting? Who the hell is he? Give me something interesting about the victims."

Amanda listened and jotted down some notes then tucked away her phone. "Alright, Nick, let's do another quick piece. I want to do as many as possible before the hawks swoop in. Let's give the other channels something to choose from."

Nick hoisted his camera back onto his shoulder. "Ready when you are."

Amanda magically transformed into her sympathetic television personality. "Amanda Harrington here for Channel Six News, where we bring you news first. We're here at Brown University as the developing tragedy unfolds. Dozens are dead or dying as the murderous madman, barricaded on top of the 16-story library, continues to fire down upon the unfortunate innocent below.

"Police confirm that this Ivy League assassin is shooting high-caliber rounds from a machine gun at an alarming rate. No one in the area is safe. He has even fired at police helicopters. Once we're able to, we will bring you footage from our own Channel Six chopper. We'll be right back with more gruesome details."

Amanda turned to the group of students who had gathered to watch the taping. "Any of you got any idea who's up there?"

Two girls pushed their redheaded friend forward. The round-faced, teary-eyed girl trembled as her friends retreated into the crowd. The girl's voice cracked. "I think it's my boyfriend."

Amanda rushed over and waved for Nick to film. Sounding concerned, she asked, "Your boyfriend is the one shooting everybody? Are you sure?"

"My ex-boyfriend. He dumped me last night."

Nick could tell that Amanda was trying not to get upset with the dumpy girl. "Are you positive that it's your ex-boyfriend?"

"Not one hundred percent, but I'm almost certain."

"Why do you think it's him?"

"He joked about doing something like this?"

"When?"

"A long time ago. Maybe a year."

"That doesn't necessarily make him the gunman."

"All his schoolwork was about violent stuff. For his sociology class he wrote about Kent State, Columbine, the Texas Tower shooting, and all kinds of crap."

"Is that it?" Amanda asked impatiently.

"No. He hated this place. He hated everyone – the students, the professors, the coaches, everyone."

"Have you seen him today?"

The girl shook her head. "Last night he said that he never wanted to see me again."

"What's his name?"

"Brandon."

"Last name?"

Nick focused on the girl. Amanda wouldn't want her viewers seeing this side of her.

"Oh, it's Taflinger."

"Do you happen to have a picture of him?"

The girl handed over her phone which displayed a photo of the couple at their Christmas formal. Nick zoomed in on the picture. The smiling young man in the tuxedo didn't look like a killer.

"Does Brandon own any guns?"

"I know he had a handgun back home. Nothing else that I knew of, though."

"Did he have any means of acquiring a weapon like the one the guy up there is using?"

"His buddy, Ken. He works over in New Jersey at the Picatinny Arsenal Army base. Brandon might have stopped by there when he went to visit his parents in New York last weekend."

They needed proof before she went on air. Amanda held up the phone and asked the distraught co-ed, "Does Brandon still look like this?"

"Yeah, except he's got a goatee now."

Amanda nodded. "Run and bring me all of his friends. Hurry. His life might depend on it."

Once the girl and her friends were gone, Amanda was back on the phone with Jonathan. "I know who he is, but I need you to verify it through the police. White male, early twenties, bald head, goatee, around six-one. Name is Brandon Taflinger. Police need to contact a person named Ken that works at Picatinny Arsenal Army Base in New Jersey. I don't have a last name for the guy, but I'm assuming he'll be 20 or 21. He's probably the one that distributed these weapons. Find out everything you can about Taflinger and the weapons, and call me back once everything is verified."

Jonathan's voice came over the earpieces that Nick and Amanda were both wearing. "From now on, I'll pass the info right over the wire in case you're filming. You're doing a hell of a job down there, Amanda. I'll let you know as soon as I get something back."

The next 45 minutes were a blur. They had several conversations with Brandon's closest acquaintances, a couple of calls from Jonathan, and two more ferocious assaults from the rooftop. Finally, Amanda was ready to go back on the air.

After a quick rehash of facts, Amanda said, "In the last few minutes, the gunman fired grenades through the windows of the computer center, killing over 56 students that were hiding inside. He also blew up a police helicopter, killing three Providence police officers in the process. The death toll has risen past 70, with as many seriously wounded, some bleeding to death because the gunman fires on anyone who tries to drag them to safety.

"I, Amanda Harrington, unraveled who this psychopath is. Channel Six will exclusively share it with you, the American public. The killer is none other than Brown University student Brandon Taflinger. Twenty-one years old. Senior. Sociology major. Caucasian male. Born and raised in a small town in upstate New York.

"It appears that Brandon's grades have been getting progressively worse each semester. As a freshman he had a 4.0 GPA, and just recently he was informed that this would be his last semester at the school due to poor grades. One reason for the declining grades could be his serious gambling problem. Over the course of the last two years, Brandon suffered incredible internet gambling losses. He incurred such a serious debt, nearly $30 thousand, that he knew he would never be able to get out of the financial hole. To make matters worse, he just lost his starting position as the varsity football team's tight end to a freshman.

"My staff uncovered that Brandon withdrew over $12 thousand in cash from his bank over the last two weeks and maxed out all of his credit cards. His bank accounts are now empty, and we believe he spent the money purchasing stolen merchandise from a friend who works at a New Jersey Army base. Authorities have already apprehended this individual, and we should find out shortly just how deadly Taflinger's arsenal is.

"You must be able to hear that in the background," Amanda shouted at the camera as gunshots and explosions rocked the muggy midafternoon. "We don't have footage, but let me tell you, it is absolute chaos out here with police returning fire on him."

The shooting ceased and Amanda held up a finger to the camera as she received a report. "Taflinger is wearing full body armor. The police sharp shooters were on target, but their bullets were deflected."

Amanda held up her finger again and listened to the conversation buzzing through her earpiece. Excitedly, she reported, "Taflinger is standing on the ledge with his back to us. He's not holding any weapons."

Amanda ripped her earpiece out and bolted around the corner. "Don't stop filming, Nick! Come on! Let's go!"

Nick shouted, "Amanda, come back! It's not safe!" She wasn't going to stop, so he jogged after her, camera rolling.

A university policeman crouching behind a tree 50 yards from the library entrance, grabbed Amanda and pulled her behind the tree despite her loud protests. Now that she was safe, Nick zoomed in on the man on the ledge.

The man did have on full body armor, but because the assailant had pulled off his facemask and helmet, Nick could see it was the kid from the picture. The report was wrong. The kid actually was holding a gun, but the police hadn't seen the 45 because it was close against his chest, pointed directly at his chin.

Nick kept the camera rolling as the twenty-one-year-old nonchalantly pulled the trigger, a fountain of blood and brain erupting from the top of his skull. The force of the shot sent his body toward the edge of the roof where it rocked briefly before plummeting toward the pavement. Taflinger had some sort of safety cable wrapped around his neck.

Taflinger tumbled through the air as the cable spooled out behind him. Nick filmed the fall and gasped when the kid reached the halfway mark and the cable went taut, instantly severing the young man's bloodied head from his body. Nick followed the body to the ground where it landed with a thunderous thud. A split second later, the decapitated head splattered on the concrete, bursting like a rotten tomato.

Nick lowered his camera and threw up his breakfast on the lawn.

Amanda pulled free from the officer and was running toward the library's entrance. "Film this, Nick! It's my story! Film it all!"

She kicked off her high heels and ran toward the headless body that lay 40 yards away. Nick wiped the vomit from his lips and resumed filming. As Amanda ran up the library's steps, Jonathan rattled off the purchases that Brandon had made from his Army buddy.

Nick dropped the camera, which fell to the pavement and shattered, and cupped his hands around his mouth megaphone-style. "Amanda! Come back! Get away from there!"

Amanda ignored him. She was going to be the only reporter to get this close to the deceased. Her beautiful face would be on every news channel in every state before the night was over.

The sight of blood didn't bother her, but the bloody heap that used to be the boy's head was a little much even for her. She took her eyes from the slushy mess and looked at the body, a river of blood cascading out of his neck. The body armor and bulky clothing had kept everything in place but she couldn't understand why there was smoke coming from the chest.

Amanda held the mic up to her mouth and turned toward Nick, infuriated he wasn't filming her. The camera was lying on the street and appeared to be broken. Before she chewed him out, she waited for him to finish his little rant.

Speaking out loud to herself, she asked, "What the hell does ten pounds of C-4 mean?"

The blasting fuse ignited the ten-pound bag of C-4 plastic explosives that was strapped around Brandon's midsection, sending a bone-shaking shockwave all the way to the bottom of the hill. Tiny bits of flesh and bone fragments were blown across the campus in a hundred-yard radius, splattering against cars, smashing into walls, flying into trees. Amanda's death made a great story for all those reporters that had wisely stayed behind the yellow police tape a mile back, fulfilling her wish to be all over the nation's news that night.

Taking Out the Trash

The bus pulls to the curb. The door opens and a fiery blast of late afternoon August air swooshes in. I hold the rail going down the stairs.

Larry waits until I'm on the sidewalk before he says, "Tell your dad I said hi." It's the same thing he says every time I get off at my stop.

I reply same as I always do, "You got it." I don't feel bad about lying because Dad would just make fun of Larry, call him a fucking loser, a lousy bus driver, a joke. And then he'd look right at me and shake his head.

Larry could tell Dad himself.

I'm not saying a word to Dad, at least not before I take out the trash. That's been my job since I was seven. It's pretty much the only thing I'm good at.

There are 59 steps from the bus stop to the corner, 32 steps across the street, 244 steps to the high school I couldn't finish, so close it is Dad's favorite reminder I'm a failure.

It takes 32 more steps to cross again, the sweat soaking the back of my coveralls and running down my crack. 142 to the house I grew up in.

It's a quiet street, most everyone in their sixties and seventies, the houses just as old and run down. Dad's is the worst, the same faded yellow peeling paint we'd had back before Mom left us 40 years ago.

Dad's rusty red pickup is parked in front of the house, the blue recycling can next to the driveway. No one else has cans out yet, and the rule is not to leave them sitting over 24 hours, but I put it there last night after I said goodbye to my old man.

As usual, the can is nearly empty, Dad not about to give away his Budweiser cans. It only contains pink and blue notification letters and white envelopes, nearly every one of them torn in half. Dad said all those citations and notices were bullshit. He owned the land and he would do whatever the hell he felt fit. The city managers could go fuck themselves because they'd never see a penny.

The baggy I pull from my pocket is only half full and there's a wet stain down the side of my pants. I almost scream at myself, but I don't need that kind of attention.

Plus, it's not a big deal. Nothing matters but the present. Take a breath and do your job, you big dummy.

I squeeze the pink cherry-scented soap from the baggy and shake it onto the papers lining the bottom, a big sploogefest as Mikey would've called it. I toss the baggy in and close the lid.

The driveway is gravel, eight steps across, and 28 more steps to the chest-high gate that's always unlocked. It's another 54 steps to the tarnished metal trashcan that sits five steps from the neighbor's wall on its little pad of concrete.

The 32-gallon trashcan is a heavy-duty monster that's been banged to hell. The first time I took out the trash, I wasn't supposed to. It was Mikey's job, but he'd just run away. Everyone said I was too little, but I knew I could do it.

Back then the trashcan was taller than me. Now I can rest my belly on it, but not today with maggots crawling everywhere. In the summer months, maggots are always a problem, especially with the mangled lid that doesn't close right and the holes in the bottom.

I fumble for the matchbook I got from Joe in a trade for one Ding-Dong. The logo for 99 Bottles is on the cover, his father's liquor store. One of the other fifth graders felt bad for me, said I could just walk in there myself and take the matches for free. I told him I don't like going in stores, especially nice ones. Plus, like Dad says, nothing ever comes free. Everything has a price.

There are 20 matches. Each burns about six seconds. Judging by the huge swarm of maggots at the bottom of the can, today could be a record-breaker.

I never told anyone what I used to do, but Dad told everyone, said I was a sick fuck for sucking the squished maggots off my thumb. No wonder Mom killed herself, he said.

The thumb sucking isn't why I squish them. I do it for the pop, to see how far the guts will go. The sucking was just me cleaning up.

I'm a pro with matches and spark one on with my thumbnail. Seven maggots shrivel in a row, five more scorched. Next match is lit and the maggots are fleeing.

Nine more melt on the lid, two burned off the handle. After two more matches my score is 23, and I've cleared the whole area.

Down below is where the numbers really add up, nowhere for the maggots to run with my big boots blocking them.

Twelve, 10, 12, 15, 11, the number keeps stacking, flecks of black dotting the ground.

Thirteen, 12, nine, two because of the wind, zero on a dud match.

I feel like a dragon scorching the land with my final five matches, the number of casualties rising past my previous record. I take a burnt tip and write 203 inside the cover then slip it into my pocket. Good luck to anyone trying to figure out if it's a clue.

Most people are surprised I can do numbers so good. I like numbers. I understand them way better than I understand people.

I was ten when I started thinking of trash days as numbers. I realized there were only going to be a certain number. Trash days only came once a week, 52 times a year.

Of course there's no knowing how short that number will be. My only friend, Jeffery Steinbach, probably thought he'd have at least 3,000 trash days, but he got cut down crossing the street when I reached number 37. Mom's number stopped before mine began, and Mikey's ended when I was 13, thanks to a bad batch of dope.

I used to think I wanted my number to go on forever, but 25 years as a custodian has given me my fill. This is it.

I assume the position, feet facing the can because I've bitten and bloodied the back of my ankles too many times, both hands on the only remaining handle.

I lift, pull, the back end scraping across the concrete, digging deep into the gravel. If Dad were watching he'd yell for me to use the dolly, don't ruin his goddamn driveway.

I glance up at the house. Every curtain is closed. Dad's not seeing shit.

So I pick up, pull, set down. Pick up, pull, set down. I get a couple of feet with each heave.

I take a break. Much as I hate to admit it, the chemo is kicking my butt. I never told Dad, didn't want to see his smile or hear his told you so.

Four heaves and I need another rest, the metal digging into my callouses, my palms purple.

The one time I asked about using gloves, Dad said if I was going to be such a girl about it, I could dig some of Alice's tampons out of the trash and reuse them.

But he was right. It made me tougher. I can handle a little pain. I can handle the weight. This day I'll show him I'm every bit the man he claims I'm not.

I make it five more heaves before I cough up a huge glob of nastiness and hock it into the bushes. Seven more heaves and I'm past the gate. I go to close it and see Fiddles lying on his side underneath the barbed bush.

I say, "Fiddles," but he's stiff as a board. He must've got into the poison. But that's okay, there's room.

I raise the lid and it smells like holy hell. I apologize to Fiddles and drop him in, get the lid on tight as I can.

The gate latches and I go back to the can, heave ho, heave ho, off to the curb we go. Well, really only six or seven feet. A few more tugs and we'll be there.

Every one of the 1,611 times I've taken out the trash I've done it the same way, both cans nice and neat against the curb, but not today. This one can stay right here in the middle of the driveway. It's too heavy to be tipped over and I'm the only person who ever visits Dad anyway.

My hands ache and my breathing's strained, but I'm happy. I'm finished. I did a good job and I did it all by myself.

Unable to resist, I raise the lid, move Fiddles to the side, gag at the mess of maggots pouring in and out of Dad's mouth.

I search my brain for something smart to say. I hock up another loogie and spit on his face. "You're right," I tell him. "We all pay a price."

The lid drops, and I go over and open the recycling bin, breathe in the cherry soap. Of the eight other houses on the block, only three driveways have cars in them. No one cares about the retard taking out the trash.

Before I chicken out, I pull the slimy razor blade from my pocket, realize I should've put it in the pocket without soap. Last night I cut a slit in my pants over the vein they say is the best to hit. I slip the razor in place and drag it up the inside of my thigh, ignore the burn, and then etch a smile across my wrist.

I lean as far as possible into the trashcan then drop inside, my face pressed into the gooey papers. It doesn't hurt much, getting light-headed as my blood oozes all around me.

1,612 is in the books, but we all end up at zero.

Exposed

In all his years of drinking, Les had never felt this bad the morning after. Or this thirsty. Even with his eyes closed, the light was too bright. He must have forgotten to close the blinds before he left to go hunting. Must've forgotten to turn on the air, too, because it was hot as hell. Actually, it was hotter than hell, and he realized he wasn't in his bed.

Les eased open his eyes, and the sun temporarily blinded him. He was lying on the desert floor, the left side of his face buried in the sand. He tried to lift his head off the ground and found it much harder than it should have been, only able to raise his head an inch.

This wasn't the first time he had blacked out and woken the next day with no recollection of the previous night, and the odds were that it wouldn't be his last. Les was many things and he hated to admit full-blown alcoholic was one of them.

He tried to push off the ground and found his hands were stuck behind his back. He wiggled this way and that, curled his hands so his fingers felt the plastic tie binding his hands together. He was handcuffed.

Les attempted to stand, but his legs were pulled toward his back, his feet shackled together by his butt and connected to his wrist. Some son of a bitch had hogtied him.

From the feel of it, it was already late morning. And late morning in Las Vegas during the third week of August was no time to be outside, especially for a redheaded Irishman. It had to be already 108 degrees and he was obviously dehydrated.

Les hated Vegas. He hated the heat, hated the desert, hated the people, hated the money. He would have stayed in Massachusetts forever if it hadn't been for his legal problems. Vegas was a big town, easy to disappear in.

He wriggled around to test the bonds and realized he was naked. He had been completely stripped, not one stitch of clothing left to cover him.

His entire right side was burnt bright red, his freckles standing out an angry dark brown. There was also something spread over his entire body. In the places that weren't covered with sand, his skin had a greasy sheen to it. It looked and smelled like baby oil. He had to get some shade soon. And some water. Goddamn he was thirsty.

His clothes weren't anywhere on the hill he had rolled down, his track obvious. No wonder his body hurt so much. He almost forgot about his headache, the right side of his head throbbing so hard it felt as if it might burst. He didn't see any rocks on the hillside that he might have hit his head on, but something had hit it. This wasn't a hangover headache.

There weren't any rocks on this side, but he hoped he could find something sharp enough to cut the plastic tie binding him. He couldn't turn around because of the way he was bound so Les threw his head back and his thighs forward in a modified Curly shuffle. Although he had barely moved, the pain was tremendous. And he had to keep doing it until he could see behind him. He couldn't just wait for someone to stumble across him.

Les jerked again. And again. He stopped and closed his eyes, trying not to throw up all over himself. He checked his surroundings, saw he had only moved half a foot, nothing but sand in sight.

Les rocked and used the momentum to drive him forward on his next jerk. Now he was moving. Sick as a dog, but moving.

The desert floor was spinning, his equilibrium upset. Last night's dinner gushed out his mouth, shooting onto the sand, wet chunks splashing back on his face and neck. The rancid smell caused him to heave again and again until nothing was left.

Les spit out the strings of vomit still in his mouth. He was extremely dehydrated, especially now, but swallowing his own puke was out of the question.

The steaming pink pool sat inches away. The chunks of undigested beef were a reminder he'd been eating a double cheeseburger and large fries while parked in his van across the street from the park. He had washed the whole meal down with an extra-large strawberry shake and countless Coors.

Everything was still a blur, but that had to be what got him in this situation. Les should have known better than to visit the same park three weeks in a row. The temptation of his past success there had been just too much to resist, and now he was paying for it.

The puke had completely dried up in under a minute. He had to escape.

Les resumed his naked Three Stooges' routine, jerking away from his undigested dinner. When he stopped and opened his eyes, he was discouraged to see there was absolutely nothing on the horizon, just mile upon mile of sand stretching as far as he could see. Whoever had rolled him down the hill must have driven him to the outskirts of the Southwest. That was one of the funny things about Vegas. Drive 50 yards down a dirt road, and next thing you know you're in the middle of the desert.

He was discouraged that he'd have to walk up the short hill, but he was relieved to see a basketball-sized boulder lying a couple of feet from his head. With any luck, he might be able to use it to cut through the tie. But first he had to get there.

After summoning his strength, Les jerked and rocked, rocked and jerked, over and over until his hands touched the scorching surface of the boulder. He had to take a break before he tried anything else. Just reaching the rock was an accomplishment.

He knew the dangers of living in the desert, had studied it before he made the miserable move. There was no doubt he was suffering from heat exhaustion. The heavy sweating, in those places where the pores weren't clogged by sand and baby oil, the weakness and tiredness, the dizziness and nausea. The muscle cramps and spasms ripping through his abdomen, arms, and legs. He'd lost so much water and salt from sweating his balls off, and he was already dehydrated from the beers. Heat stroke couldn't be too far off.

The practical joke or whatever it was had gone from being a major pain in the ass to a life-threatening emergency. He could die if he got heat stroke. He needed water. He needed shade. He needed to get the fuck out of his restraints.

Even though the pain in his shoulders was nearly unbearable and his skin was being rubbed raw on the scorching sand, Les moved back and forth, up and down, in a continuous circle, furiously rubbing the plastic tie over the sharpest edge of the rock. The fiery lactic acid buildup inside his shoulders soon matched the blazing intensity of the sun. Finally, the tie frayed. A few more seconds of rubbing broke it completely.

Les flexed his legs over and over to pump blood into them. He dug his heels into the burning sand and pushed himself upright, ignored the dizziness and the new wave of nausea. The outer half of his right leg was lobster-red with a couple patches blistering.

Les tried to get his hands in front of him by slipping them under his butt, but he was too inflexible. He found the rock with his fingers and maneuvered the sharp edge against the plastic binding his wrists. Even the thinnest part of the rock was too thick for the job, and it rubbed against both wrists.

Ever so slowly, Les moved his hands back and forth over the rock, ignoring the layers of skin peeling off his wrists. He picked up the pace and felt the tie give a little, his work lubricated by the blood seeping through the scrapes.

Les looked for some kind of marker over the top of the hill. Depending on which way he was facing, he should be able to see the top of a casino, part of a high-rise, something. All he could see was the oppressive, clear blue sky. It didn't matter because a minute later his hands were free, wrists bleeding onto his lap, but free. Now all he had to do was get his legs free and he could get out of this hellhole.

The cuts on his wrist weren't deep enough to be life threatening. But what worried him were his arms. He usually sweated like a pig, but now there wasn't a drop on him. Not on his arms. Not on his forehead. Nowhere. Heat exhaustion was progressing to heat stroke.

There was a huge bump on the right side of his throbbing head. When he brought his hand down, his fingers were spotted with sticky blood. Whoever had bound him had beat him, but he didn't know who or why.

Les used the bloody rock to saw through the tie binding his feet and tried to remember what had happened the previous night. The pile of puke reminded him he'd been eating in the van while he waited. He had been waiting for a long time. There had been a lot of kids coming and going from the park, but they were all in groups.

Things started to come back to him. He'd polished off a whole 12 pack when the car pulled in behind him. If he'd been smart, he would have taken off immediately, but there were some good prospects playing on the swings. They were a little younger than he usually preferred, but he was so horny that he was anxious to grab anyone. And he didn't even have to do anything with them. Even if he only flashed one or two kids, he would have been okay until the next week, or at least three or four days.

The rock sawed through the tie and bit into his ankles, ripping Les out of the memory. He tossed the rock and got to his knees. The hill was only about five times his height, but steep enough to instill doubt about his ability to scale it.

To quench his thirst and get some fluid in his dry mouth, Les put both wrists against his parched lips and sucked. The blood was salty and warm but it was liquid, something wet to clear the sand and puke. It would have to be enough to get him to the top of the hill. After that he could walk to a house or flag down a car. Someone would help him.

Every step was torture. The sun was directly overhead. The sand was fire. The incline, a wall. But he had to keep going.

Using his hands as his guide, Les closed his eyes and climbed the incline like a bear. Eyes closed, the dizziness minimized, he took his mind off his body and returned to the night before. It was the car that pulled up behind him. The guy that got out. The cop. A cop did this.

The memory was still fuzzy, but he remembered looking through his side mirror and seeing the cop creep alongside the van. By that time it was too late to run, but Les had time to get his ID ready. At least he thought he did. When he closed the glovebox and sat back in his seat, the cop was staring at him through the window.

The cop hadn't bought the fake ID and demanded to see the wallet, which Les handed over. Upon the discovery of Les' real driver's license tucked away behind some business cards, the cop ordered Les out of the van and had him wait in the patrol car while he ran his info. Sitting in the backseat, Les had been worried about violating parole. When the cop drove a few blocks away to the deserted area behind the park, he ordered Les out of the car. Les should have known he had more to worry about than being sent back east.

Les opened his eyes and saw he had almost reached the top. A few more feet and he'd be on level ground, probably less than 50 yards from salvation. Les misjudged his next step and his right foot slid out from under him. His body slammed down onto the sand, his chest and groin scraping along the gritty landscape as he dropped several feet.

He turned his head to the side and tried to spit out a mouthful of sand. He wasn't going to make it. The lip of the hill was only five yards up, but those were the longest five yards he had ever seen.

Just as he was about to call it quits, he heard someone shout his nickname, Moe. It couldn't be though. No one in Nevada knew his nickname. Ever since he was a kid, everyone had called him Moe. Not his mom or sisters, of course. They always called him Leslie, which he absolutely hated, or Lester when he was in trouble for trying on their makeup or stealing their clothes; but all the kids at school called him Moe as if they knew something he didn't.

Les crawled toward the angelic voice, buried his hands deep into the sand and pulled himself up a foot at a time. His shoulders and upper arms twitched like crazy, and he would have scars to last a lifetime, but he was going to make it. That bastard cop had taught him a lesson. That was the last time he'd stalk prey at a park. And he was getting out of Nevada. If he never saw the sun again, it would be just fine with him.

With one last lunge, Les pulled himself over the top of the hill. He had made it. Now all he had to do was make it to a store, find someone, get some clothes, some shade, some water, a hospital. But he'd made it.

Les raised his head and looked to see which way to go. There was nothing in front of him. Nothing to either side. Nothing behind him. No savior calling his name.

The desert floor stretched for mile after mile, sand and cactus the only things visible. Les collapsed, barely aware of the blazing sand burning into his cheek, his chest, his crotch. A few feet ahead, taped to a boulder, was a plastic Metro police department pamphlet. Les had to concentrate to read the slogan, "Cleaning up the community, one criminal at a time."

The Fine Print

Mr. Cohen handed Stan and Gary their contracts, then laid his folded hands on his mahogany desk. Cohen's black suit, blue tie, crisp white shirt, and manicured hands screamed class, but the look was a bit too stuffy for Stan. Stan looked great in a suit, but he'd rather throw on a nice pair of jeans and a snug polo so he wouldn't be too intimidating to women who might want to approach him.

"Gentlemen, before we get started, let me just make certain that you understand how this works. This is mediation, not arbitration. There is no judge or jury; just the two of you talking out your differences, with me helping you come to a satisfactory resolution."

Anxious to get it over with, Stan said, "We got it."

"Gary, how about you? Any questions?"

Not surprisingly, Gary shook his head, unable to assert himself and speak even a one-word answer.

"Then if you would both please review the contract and sign and date it. Today is the thirtieth."

Stan turned to the back of the ten-page contract. "What exactly am I signing here? Not promising my first born or anything like that?" he joked, flashing his winning smile and turning the charm on, already trying to get Cohen in his corner.

"It simply states that the resolution you reach is binding and cannot be appealed. It also waives your right to sue Final Solution if things don't go the way you expected them to."

Stan put pen to paper, chuckling as he scrawled his name. "Not too worried about that."

"I recommend that you read the whole thing."

Stan flipped through the pages to satisfy Cohen. "Looks like your standard contract. I'd like to get this thing started if we could."

Stan looked to his right. Gary was on page three. "Come on, man. I don't have all day."

"He can take as long as he needs."

Predictably, Gary folded under Stan's pressure and turned to the last page. After carefully signing his name, he handed the contract to Cohen. Speaking to Stan, but looking straight ahead, he asked, "Happy?"

Stan slid his contract across the desk to the mediator. "Very. Let's start."

Cohen held up a finger as he checked the signatures. Stan was tempted to reach across the desk and snap the pretentious prick's finger in two, but instead he sat there with a smile pasted on his face.

"One more thing," Cohen said as he looked up from the contracts. "I'll need both of your watches and cell phones."

Stan looked down at his Cartier and shook his head. "I don't think so."

"It's one of my rules. No phones, clocks, watches, or hourglasses. Once this thing is started we don't finish until we've reached a satisfactory conclusion."

Gary handed over his phone and cheap Timex. Stan took his time unclasping his watch. Cohen took it from him and walked to a paneled wall. When he pushed the middle section of the wall, a panel slid to the side revealing a safe. With his back blocking their view, Cohen dialed in the combination, opened the safe, and inserted the contracts and their belongings. Before closing the safe, Cohen pushed a button that unlocked the hidden door next to it.

Stan pretended to be impressed. "Wow. Look at you, all *Mission Impossible*."

Cohen pulled the door open and motioned for the men to head down the dimly lit concrete hallway. "Not exactly. We just respect our clients' privacy. And can you really blame me for not wanting this ugly door in the middle of my office?"

Stan glanced about the plush office. "You've got a point. Plus, people would be wondering where that door went instead of listening to what you were saying."

Gary, who had just entered the hallway, took the bait. "Where does it go?"

Cohen took off his jacket and hung it on the back of his chair. "Last door on the left."

Stan strode down the long hallway, breathing down Gary's back. When Gary stepped into the room and stopped abruptly, Stan stumbled and collided into Gary's back.

"What the hell, dickweed? Why'd you stop?"

"You should watch where you're going," Gary said under his breath.

"Enough of that." Cohen walked between the two men. "Gary, have a seat over there," he said, pointing to the edge of the sunken concrete pit that filled the room. "Stan, you take that side."

Stan looked where Cohen was pointing. "Are you serious? There's no cushion."

"Take a seat, Stan."

Gary walked to his side of the pit, stepped into it and sat on the edge. Stan went to his side and plopped down onto the hard concrete. Trying to make light of the uncomfortable situation, he said, "Fill this thing with water and we've got ourselves one hell of a Jacuzzi. I'll line up the cooze, if you handle the booze."

"I thought you wanted to get started, Stan?" Cohen's dry, monotone voice was starting to grate on Stan's nerves.

Stan looked away from Cohen and caught Gary smirking. He restrained himself from dashing across the eight feet that divided them and smashing him in the face. "What's so funny, you little pencil-neck geek?"

Cohen stepped to the edge of the pit. "Stan, that's the last time you insult Gary without there being a consequence. Understood?"

"Don't speak to me like I'm a child."

"Don't act like one."

Stan's blood was boiling. He didn't trust himself to look at Cohen, but staring across at Gary was almost as bad.

"Now if you two are ready to start, please place your feet on the markings in front of you."

The outlines of two feet were painted on the concrete floor a few inches away from the step. When Stan placed his feet inside the markings, two metal shackles shot out from the wall inside the pit and clasped both ankles. He jumped to his feet and nearly fell over as the restraints prevented him from moving forward.

"Easy, Stan," Cohen said. "It's part of the session. They don't hurt, do they?"

Stan looked across at Gary who was sitting there, acting as if the ankle chains didn't bother him. He sat back down on the concrete ledge. Speaking to Cohen, he said, "You could have warned us."

"Relax, Stan," Gary said. "They're not going to hurt you."

Cohen pressed the intercom on the wall and said, "We're ready." A few moments later, the door across the hall opened and two men with wheelbarrows full of wood entered the mediation room. The two men placed their wheelbarrows at the edge of the sunken pit and constructed a three-foot-high pile of logs directly between Gary and Stan.

The two workers left the room with their empty wheelbarrows. Stan joked, "Where are the marshmallows?"

"Sorry, Stan, but we don't provide any treats."

Trying not to sound nervous, but smelling the familiar scent of lighter fluid, Stan asked, "So what's all this?"

"It's our way of teaching you both a valuable lesson. Each time one of you says something negative about the other, you are adding fuel to the fire instead of putting it out. Some people have difficulty grasping that concept. Here at Final Solution, we have made it a little more real."

The two workers came back with wheelbarrows overflowing with wood and set them on either side of Cohen. One placed a large fire extinguisher next to Cohen's feet.

Stan thought the whole idea was stupid, but he would play along. "Oh, I get it. As soon as I say something about him, you light the fire."

Cohen pulled a lighter from his suit and flicked the flame on. "You're exactly right."

"Hold on a second. You can't be serious," Gary said, squirming away from the pile of logs. "I'm out of here."

"So you're willing to let all of your claims go? You're going to give the business to Stan?"

"Yeah, Gary, just give it to me. You know I should have it anyway."

Gary settled down. "I'm not giving you anything."

"Good," Cohen said, still holding the burning lighter. "It'd be such a waste setting all this up for nothing. Discuss your problems like rational men. Let's come to a resolution."

"Hate to tell you this, but I wouldn't call threatening to set a fire between us as being the most rational thing I've ever seen."

"Stan, we've never had a case come to an unsatisfactory conclusion. What other mediator can promise a one hundred percent success rate?"

"Then let's do it. This smell is giving me a headache." Stan looked across the mound of logs. "You ready, weasel-boy?"

Cohen tossed the lighter onto the pile, setting it ablaze. He pressed a button on the wall, turning on the exhaust fans installed above the pit. Cohen faced them with a smile. "I told you that the next negative comment would have consequences. We have started, gentlemen, and we'll continue until we've finished."

"You're crazy!" Stan backed away as far the restraints allowed. "What the hell do you think you're doing? These clothes are going to be ruined!"

Cohen slipped on a pair of black leather gloves, picked up a log from the wheelbarrow closest to Stan and tossed it onto the fire.

Trying not to let his temper get the best of him, Stan said, "I didn't say anything about him."

"You can't get mad at anyone but yourself," Cohen said smugly. "The two of you have the power to end this. I recommend doing it quickly."

Stan used the back of his forearm to wipe the sweat from his forehead. He looked down and saw that the tips of his four-hundred-dollar shoes were melting. He bent over, picked up the end of a burning log and tossed it at Cohen. "Turn this shit off and let me the fuck out of here before I sue the hell out of you guys."

Cohen picked up the extinguisher and sprayed the burning log by his feet. "You probably should have taken a closer look at the contract. Always read the fine print, Stan."

Stan reached for a log, but his hands came too close to the fire. The lighter fluid that had rubbed off on him from the log he'd tossed ignited, and he threw his blazing hands into the air. Screaming in pain, he looked at Cohen who was standing there with the extinguisher.

"What do you say?"

"Please!" Stan yelled. "Please put it out!"

Cohen put out the fire on Stan's hands, covering the entire front of his body with the white foam. "That's a freebie. No more Mr. Nice Guy. I suggest you two get started."

Stan started to object, but Gary said, "I think we should talk, Stan. Come on, I'm scared."

Stan ripped off his shirt and wrapped it around his smoldering hands, hoping to ease the pain. "What the fuck you want to talk about? You put me in here, you goddamned Jew."

Cohen tossed another log onto Stan's side.

"What'd I say now?"

"Personal attacks won't help you come to a satisfactory resolution."

"He's not even Jewish. It's just an expression. Jews are known for being cheap."

"Thanks, but I'm well aware of that stereotype."

Gary said, "It's fine. Let's just talk and get this over with. It's starting to burn my legs." Gary looked to Cohen and asked, "Can't we just stop this? We understand."

Cohen pointed to the yellow button next to the intercom. "That unlocks your restraints. Come to a satisfactory resolution and I will press it."

Gary said, "You backdoored me and stole my major accounts, ones I had before we even started our partnership. Now it looks like I'm not bringing anything to the table. My take-home pay is half of yours."

"Is that why you're stealing?"

Gary didn't answer. Cohen picked up a log and asked Gary, "Is that a true accusation or a false attack?"

When Gary didn't answer, Cohen threw a log on each side of the blaze.

"Answer him, you prick," Stan said as he nudged away a burning log. "You know you're stealing."

"I had to. You took all my accounts," Gary said with a whine.

"You weren't servicing them right. If you had, maybe your clients wouldn't have approached me."

"I didn't service them right?"

"That's what I said."

Gary looked defeated when he asked, "Like my wife, you son of a bitch? Is that why you slept with her?" It was impossible to tell if it was tears or sweat rolling down his cheeks.

Cohen threw two logs onto Gary's side of the pyre. "Sit and calm yourself."

Stan smiled even though he could barely see Gary's deflated face through the rising flames. Unable to stop himself, Stan said, "If it makes you feel any better, we never did any sleeping."

Gary cried out and jumped to his feet, forgetting about the ankle restraints and raging fire in front of him. He fell face first onto the inferno and panicked, throwing logs out of his way. His shirt was on fire when he got back on his feet.

Cohen doused him with the extinguisher and told him to sit. Once Gary was seated, Cohen threw two more logs onto Gary's side and tossed the extinguisher behind him. "No more chances. You two better hurry."

Seeing his partner on fire sobered Stan. Trying to regain control of the situation, he said, "I'm sorry, Gary, but I didn't exactly rape her."

Speaking so low that Stan could barely hear him over the crackling fire, Gary said, "You were screwing my wife in my own office."

"She seduced me. You know she's not my type. You've seen the girls I've been with. I like them young and tight, not middle age and saggy."

Cohen tossed two logs onto Stan's side. They caught fire and rolled onto Stan's shoes, setting his jeans on fire. Stan brought his shirt-wrapped hands to his pants and slapped the fire out.

"I didn't say anything!" Stan yelled, knowing he wouldn't survive many more logs.

"Stan!" Gary shouted. "Let's agree on something. Hurry up. My pants are melting!"

Stan kicked at the burning logs and set his jeans on fire again. "Put me out, you fuck!" he ordered Cohen.

Cohen stepped behind Stan's wheelbarrow and grabbed the handles. Stan whipped his head back to Gary, whom he could no longer see. "Sell me the business for two hundred thousand, plus you keep ten percent."

Gary cowered in a heap of sobbing moans.

The fire seared his calves and climbed his legs. "You miserable Jew!"

Cohen heaved on the handles and dumped the logs into the pit. Within seconds, the flames licked the ceiling, engulfing Stan's legs. Barely able to think, Stan shouted, "We'll never agree! There's no solution!"

"There's always a solution," Cohen said as he turned toward the door. "And this one is fine by me."

Left Behind

The sun threatened to disappear behind the cafeteria, but Ben kept swinging back and forth, his shoes gliding across the sand at the bottom of his arc. If he stared at the sun long enough, maybe he'd go blind like his mom warned. Then he wouldn't have to open the envelope and look inside. If he was blind, he wouldn't have to see his report card, find out if he'd been left behind once again.

There wasn't anything for Ben to see out there anyhow. If he went blind, he wouldn't miss a thing. Except for all the trash flitting about, the playground was empty. Everyone was gone, off to their parties, glad eighth grade was over, excited for high school.

The swing slowed, and Ben concentrated on the sun instead of the orange and green Silly String sprayed across the buildings. Going blind might help him forget the yells of celebration at the final bell, the jerks telling him to say hi to Miss Dykstra next year when he was back in her English class. He opened his eyes as wide as possible and watched the sun sink, pretending he didn't mind not being invited to any parties. He kept looking at the sun, happy when everything became dark, only to realize it was because the sun had set.

Ben pushed off the sand and began swinging again, trying not to care that he'd never been invited to the parties. Not the first time. Not last year. Not today.

Even if the report card was horrible, if they said he was too stupid to go to high school, maybe it wouldn't be so bad. The eighth graders were mean, calling him a loser, dumbshit, moron, fucking retard. They'd only get nastier as freshmen.

Ben wiped his eyes, yelping when his scraped knuckle brushed against his bruised cheek. There was nothing across the darkened playground except scattered papers floating about like little ghosts. There was no one around to hear him, see him swinging by himself, wonder why he was out at night and why Andy wasn't with him.

Everything was quiet, but that was okay. Ben wasn't afraid of the silence, not like some kids. When it was quiet, it meant he couldn't hear anyone laughing at him.

His size 13 boots scraped the sand beneath him as he thought about how it wouldn't be so bad to have his teachers again. Miss Angie let him eat his granola bars whenever he was hungry, as long as he didn't crunch too loud. Mr. Thomas didn't ask him questions or make him stand up in front of the class and talk like he did the other kids. And Miss Dykstra would keep letting him take home the test so he could study real hard and stop ruining the curve, whatever that was.

There was only one thing that Ben would miss, and that was the reason he was fighting these little-boy tears. He would miss Andy, his best friend. His only friend. Ever. But not anymore. Not after the fight they'd had.

Ben shook his head and sand flew off his hair. He didn't want to think about the brawl. He wanted to remember Andy for being a good friend. He wanted to remember him as the boy that didn't laugh at him, call him names, push him down and tease him. Andy was the only kid who didn't make fun of his stutter, who didn't laugh when Ben got the answers wrong or mixed up his words. Andy was the only one who talked to Ben at lunch time, who told him not to worry about the other kids, that they were the dumb ones. But today Andy was the one who had said something stupid. He said something stupid about Ben's mom. And Ben got mad. And then they fought. And now Ben had no friends again.

The wind picked up a piece of paper and blew it onto Ben's chest. Trying not to get blood on it when he held it in front of him, Ben attempted to read the name at the top. He only made out the M and A before giving up on the rest of it. The name didn't matter. What mattered was that the paper had an A plus on it. Someone threw away an A plus. If Ben ever had a B, it would be on his fridge forever.

Ben let the wind pull the paper from his hand and blow it behind him where he wouldn't see it ever again. The grade reminded him of his report card. He had to look at it. He should have opened it when Andy told him to. Then none of this would have happened, and they'd still be friends.

Before he chickened out, Ben took the envelope from his back pocket and ripped it open. He tapped the report card free, prayed there would be no F's. His mom said he had to pass all his classes or he wouldn't be able to live with his dad anymore and he'd be sent somewhere else and never see her again. She said neither of them had the money to send him to a special school. Andy said they did. Said she could sell her fucking BMW. Said she could put Ben in a good school if she wanted to.

Ben tried not to think about the things Andy said and focused on the report card. His full name, the one he wanted to use but his dad wouldn't let him because Ben sounded stupid when he tried to say Benjamin, was at the top of the card. The classes were below that. He couldn't read all the names, but he knew what the big letters next to them meant. Those were the grades. The ones that decided his future. They were all C's.

"The teachers passed me." He wished Andy could see it. Ben held the report card high, the blood dripping off his knuckle and falling to the dark sand. "I'm ready for high school."

Ben pushed off the sand, swinging a little higher, trying to make himself feel better. He should've been happy, shouting out to the world that he'd finally passed all his classes. He wasn't a loser.

But Ben wasn't happy. Andy was gone. He couldn't tell him the good news.

Ben's feet dragged beneath him, carving a ditch in the sand, slowing him down. Andy had no right to say mean things about Ben's mom, even if he said them to make Ben stop crying. He shouldn't have called her a bad mom.

If Ben had just plugged his ears and talked real loud, then he wouldn't have heard Andy say, "Screw your mom." That all Ben's mom did was make him sad. That she only called Ben once a month and she lied to him, saying she would visit and take him somewhere and then never show up and then Ben would mope around all day.

The words wouldn't come out, and Ben got frustrated when he tried to tell Andy that his mom had her reasons. That was when Andy said she was a bitch. And then Ben couldn't think right anymore, and everything went kind of fuzzy and red.

The swing jolted to a stop when Ben's foot struck something. He had kicked a blue Nike sneaker free from the sand.

Ben got off the swing and crouched beside the shoe. After carefully brushing it off, he slipped the sneaker back on the sock sticking out of the sand, then scooped giant armloads of sand on top of it, covering it all up so no one would ever, ever find it. He didn't want Miss Angie yelling at him for fighting with Andy. Ben knew fighting was wrong. She'd tell him he knew better than that.

After taking one last look at the lump beneath the swing, Ben got to his feet, brushed the sand off his clothes and walked across the playground. The report card in his hand should have made him happy, but he couldn't be happy knowing that this year it was Andy's turn to be left behind.

The Mirror

Father Gabriel trembled on the edge of his bed, his eyes fixed on the oversized floor mirror. Never before had he seen a beast so vile, its scaly skin the scarlet hue of an opened artery. The demonic creature grinned at him from inside the reflective surface and slid its bloated tongue across inch-long incisors. Bubbling ebony blood dribbled down the monster's chin and onto its massive chest.

Frozen on the bed, each breath forced, the priest prayed for strength. Father Gabriel knew there couldn't be a monster in the mirror, but he couldn't deny the features of the room were exactly as they should be. The cluttered desk in the corner. The painting on the wall hanging slightly askew. Light snow falling outside the window. The only difference was the winged demon sitting on the bed where he himself should have been.

The evil monster had to be a figment of his imagination. Father Gabriel had never questioned his sanity, but maybe he'd gone mad from the lack of sleep and all the stress. Watching his mother wither away over the last six months had taxed him terribly. The worst was taking her to chemo sessions and lying to her each time, telling her she'd be okay. It wasn't fair to her and it wasn't fair to him. It was an unjust reward for his 30 years of dedicated service to the Lord.

Insanity wasn't an attractive option, but neither was Satan revealing one of his minions, proving he was much more powerful than Father Gabriel had dreamed possible. He preached about the evil on Earth every Sunday, but he had always interpreted it figuratively. He didn't really believe demons roamed the earth, and not once did he expect to see one materialize in front of him.

Father Gabriel tested the reflection with a wave of his hand, and the demon copied him, blood dripping off its razor-sharp claws. The priest shook his head in disbelief, and the demon whipped his own from side to side, his piercing eyes and gnashing teeth glistening in the light.

It was a soul snatcher, no doubt, but that gave the priest hope. Father Gabriel was not without sin, and his heart was heavy with guilt, but surely not dark enough to sustain the demon.

A knowing smile spread like a disease across the horrid face. The demon's jaw unhinged and opened wide, a fiery glow brightening the back of its throat. A scarlet steam gathered on the mirror, then transformed into a misty red light flowing down the demon's throat.

The demon had to be eating away his guilt, because as frightened as he was, Father Gabriel felt freer with each passing moment. No longer did he feel guilty for wishing he had siblings to share the burden of taking care of his mother, nor did his conscience suffer for not spending more time with her. After all, he visited every morning and had just returned from her place less than an hour before. Gone was the guilt for regretting he'd become a priest in the first place. If he'd gotten a real job, he could have afforded to place his mother in a nice retirement community instead of leaving her to rot away in her roach-infested apartment.

The only guilt that remained was over the stupid mirror. Mr. Kerrington had told him he could take whatever he wanted from the house in exchange for absolving his sins. Even when Father Gabriel assured Kerrington that his sins would be forgiven regardless, the old man insisted. Kerrington had no heirs, and all his belongings would be given to the state. As he spoke his last words, Kerrington made the priest promise to take something.

Mirrors had never been of any interest to Father Gabriel, who spent his childhood constantly reminded he was lacking in the looks department, but something about this one had drawn him closer. The exquisite craftsmanship and intricate detail were undeniable, a valuable piece of art worth more than all of Father Gabriel's possessions combined. His vow of poverty had been for nothing, his mother all the proof he needed. He deserved the mirror.

After hearing the blood-chilling atrocities Kerrington confessed to having committed in his master bedroom where the mirror stood, Father Gabriel should have known better. With awareness of his impending death, but no sign of remorse, Kerrington thoroughly detailed the brutalities he'd inflicted over the course of a century. He had tortured countless animals, draining them of life and bathing in their blood. He'd kidnapped young children and brought them to his lair, only to break their bodies and spirits. The old man spent his entire life worshipping the dark lord, destroying his loved ones, even offering some as sacrifice.

Father Gabriel had been reckless in taking anything from that cursed house, let alone that evil bedroom. The mirror had witnessed unfathomable wickedness, but Father Gabriel had felt he must have it. Something in the mirror called out to him. Now that there was a demon laughing at him, mimicking his every movement, he wondered if the demon had tricked him into bringing it into a house of worship. Had Kerrington been serving Satan to the end, passing evil from his house to one of God's?

In the distance, Father Gabriel heard the rectory telephone ringing. There were murmurs, footsteps, then a knock at his door. When he didn't answer, the knock sounded again. Still, he couldn't speak, couldn't take his eyes off the mirror, the trail of red flowing through the mirror and down the demon's throat.

After another unanswered knock, the rectory secretary let herself into the bedroom. "I'm so sorry to bother you, Father, but you have a phone call," Margaret said from the doorway, her voice shaking. "I'm afraid there's some bad news. It's about your mother."

The demon stared Father Gabriel dead in the eye and gave a knowing wink.

"It's Janet, the hospice worker. She's hysterical," Margaret said. "Can you talk to her? I really think you should."

Margaret stepped into the room. Still gazing into the mirror, Father Gabriel could see the tears welling in the woman's eyes. She was a good person. He didn't want her to see the demon and witness Satan's power, but he was petrified with fear, unable to stop her from coming closer. Father Gabriel shuddered to think what it would do to Margaret if it escaped its glass prison.

"You need to speak with her, Father."

He tried to talk, but the demon wouldn't let him.

Tears coursed down her cheeks. "I'm sorry, but your mother is dead."

Part of him had been expecting this call, almost wishing for it, but now that it was here, he didn't feel the relief he had anticipated. Still, he had to be strong. Watching the monster mouth his words, he steadied his voice and said, "It's okay, Margaret. She's with God now."

"No, you don't understand. She didn't go peacefully." Margaret took a deep breath. "She was beaten to death. Janet said she could barely recognize her."

Father Gabriel ran his hands through his snow-white hair and groaned. The demon clutched its horns and chuckled.

Margaret gasped, one hand clutching the phone to her chest, the other pointing at the priest. "Oh my God!"

He changed his mind about her witnessing the monstrosity. "Thank the Lord. You see it too."

"Your hair. There's blood in it." She looked down. "Your knuckles are bleeding. What happened? Are you okay?"

Father Gabriel broke the mirror's spell and looked where his hands should have been. In their place, the demon's clenched fists dripped his mother's blood onto the hardwood floor.

Counting on It

Blake had read all the directives, watched all the videos, and signed all the waivers; but he never thought this could happen to him. He was lying on the office floor with a throbbing puncture through his palm, a jagged gash down his forearm, and a dime-sized hole in his shoulder.

His emergency situation training was a blur. Never look away from the subject because it shows fear, or was it never make eye contact to show your compliance? Do you question his authority or challenge it, demand he listen or beg for mercy? Damn it, if only he had paid attention.

Blake kept his eyes on the oversized teenager hovering over him. "Put it down, Teddy. Please put it down. I won't fight."

In his annoyingly slow monotone, Teddy said, "Kill number one was Manny. Manny the nanny. He did girl job."

The initial shock was wearing off, and Blake's wounds hurt like hell. Teddy must have hit a vein in his shoulder because it was flowing freely. Even if the dumb bastard didn't stab him again, Blake was in danger of bleeding out. Time for a new tactic. "As your doctor I'm commanding you to stop this. Put the shank down."

Teddy waved the piece of rusty metal back and forth. "Manny liked boys."

"That's not why you killed him."

"I know that." He jabbed playfully at Blake's face, made him cringe against the wall. "Fifteen-year-olds don't have babysitters. I was bigger, too."

Much bigger. Teddy was a solid 220 pounds. His size combined with the mental ability of a first-grader made for a scary package. "I saw the pictures. Put it down, Teddy. Let's talk."

"He said 'love.'" Teddy looked through Blake with his vacant blue eyes. "I bashed his head and he stopped ticking."

"Let me up, Teddy. Let me sit in my chair. We can talk about Manny."

"Mommy and Daddy were mad for him not being there when they got home. I said he went with his boyfriend. They didn't look in the garage."

"You think that's funny?"

"It is." He grinned from ear to ear and struck downward, the sharpened scrap of metal tearing through Blake's slacks and into his calf.

Blake screamed, but no one was around to hear it. The office was at the end of the deserted wing. Bob was the only one who knew they were in here. And Bob wouldn't be helping out anytime soon.

"Jesus, Teddy. Stop that so we can talk."

Teddy wiped the blood onto the front of his orange state-issued sweatshirt and held up his thumb and index finger. "Two was Granddaddy. He said batteries. Had a real small one in his heart. How stupid. One battery can't make a person tick. My race car has four and it stops ticking after one day. I showed him when I held the bag over his head."

Teddy could understand the concept of batteries dying but still couldn't wrap his pea-sized brain around his stupid little question, the one no one had answered correctly thus far. Blake told him, "That was wrong. You know that deep down."

"He was wrong."

Blake had a difficult time talking through his tears. "That's not what I meant. Why don't you put that on the table?"

"Why don't you stop crying?"

"I don't want to die."

"Tell me the answer."

"There is no right answer."

Teddy stared at the three fingers he was holding up. "Three. Grandpa's nurse, Ms. Jelly, said she knew. That's not her real name but I like to say it. Jelly belly. I like Jelly Bellies and she has a big belly."

"Why'd you kill Ms. Kelly? What did she answer?"

"She said heart. I didn't even cut near her heart."

"You slit her throat."

"Don't talk to me like I don't know anything. I hate it when people treat me special."

This was the first time Teddy showed real anger. Blake had to tread carefully. "You are special."

"I'm average."

"Why do you say that? Who taught you that?"

"You did. You said I got 71 on my test. In school I never got that high. Seventy-one is a C."

Blake sighed. "That was an IQ test, Teddy."

"I have average IQ."

Blake groaned. "I explained that to you. It's well below average."

"You sure?" Teddy jabbed Blake twice in the stomach.

"Stop it, Teddy! Jesus Christ. Put that thing down. I'm sorry. I'm just trying to explain."

Teddy wiped more blood onto his sweatshirt. "Number four lied. Momma said family."

"That was no reason to throw the curling iron in the bathtub."

"Rest of family was still alive when she stopped ticking. She lied."

"You killed her before your father? He didn't hear anything?"

"Drunk was asleep. Didn't wake until whole bed was on fire." Teddy imitated his father's death throes and said, "He was all like this. Like he was swimming in the air. But screaming."

Blake's strength had diminished greatly and he was having trouble concentrating. "Can I sit in my chair, Teddy?"

"I'm talking bout five."

"Five?"

He held out all five fingers on his left hand. "Daddy was five. He said money. His money was on the dresser when he stopped tick-tock-tick-tock-ticking."

Blake might still have a chance if he could remember how many people Teddy had killed. Blake stalled by saying, "You know that money doesn't keep us alive. Why did you really kill him?"

"To show he lied. He said money."

"You need to understand the difference between literal and figurative. I know they're big words and hard to understand, but you need to try."

"I don't need to do nothing. I give rules now."

"You do. I'm sorry. I'm listening, Teddy. You don't need the shank anymore. I won't try to do anything. I promise."

Still holding the weapon with his four fingers, Teddy extended his thumb and concentrated on how many fingers he was holding up. "Six. That was Mikey. He lied. Said girls. He didn't say girls but I know that's what he meant. He said bad word for naughty place down there."

"Did you hate your brother? He teased you a lot, didn't he?"

"He lied. There were no girls around when he stopped ticking."

"What about Stacy? Wasn't she home?"

"In the other room. Not for long."

"Why'd you kill her?"

"She said beauty. I cut her face 40, 50, 60 times. She had no more beauty but kept ticking. She stopped when I held her down in the bathtub with Mommy. That way they could be together."

"What number was she?"

Teddy stopped wobbling side to side and looked as if his mind temporarily shut down. After a few seconds of silence, he smiled and held up seven fingers, the grip on his weapon not very secure.

If the numbers were right, Blake might get out of the situation. Teddy was unable to count past ten, said there was no higher number. Ten was the ultimate number, the highest there ever could be. When Blake had challenged him on it during their first session, Teddy had gone into a nearly catatonic state and wasn't coaxed out of it for nearly an hour.

"Teddy, can you calm down so we can talk for a minute? I want to help you figure things out."

"Then tell me the answer. Don't lie."

"I can think better if you put that down. Just put it on the table so we can talk. I want to talk to you."

"You have no choice. You're gonna talk."

"Please put it down. If you put it down and let me off the floor, we can have a normal conversation like rational adults."

"Rational?"

"You're capable of rational thought. We had a great conversation last session."

"Courts said I'm not. Are you smarter than the judge?"

Blake was surprised by Teddy's reasoning, but not pleased with the way he was leading the conversation. "I'm not saying that."

"So what are you saying?"

"I'd like for both of us to sit in our chairs and talk about what happened."

"That's what I'm doing. Number eight was policeman. Couldn't ask him before I stabbed him. No time."

The cop had been the last one on Teddy's killing spree. Eight wasn't enough. "Did you know he had a family? You killed him and it had nothing to do with your question."

Teddy swung the shank in a wide arc, the tip ripping through Blake's shirt and tearing a path across his chest.

"I'm sorry, I'm sorry! It's not stupid. I didn't mean that. I meant to say it isn't a fair question." The front of Blake's shirt was bright crimson. He had to do something quick, but he was already so weak. "There is no real answer. No one can answer that question correctly."

Teddy set the bloody shank on the desk and held up nine fingers. "Adam thought he could. He snored loud. He said we have gears like a watch."

"Adam was severely retarded."

"I ripped him apart all night. Couldn't find one piece of metal."

Teddy wasn't exaggerating. When the orderly entered their room the next morning, he slipped on the blood-slick floor and landed on top of the mutilated teenager. They never found the weapon, but Blake figured it had to be the one Teddy was now wielding.

"Where'd you hide it?"

"Laundry bin. Wrapped in dirty underwear. No one looks there."

"Very smart." Too smart for someone with his IQ.

Teddy fanned all his fingers. "Ten, ten, ten. I did ten." He nodded toward the far corner. "He's ten."

Blake had blocked out Bob so thoroughly that he hadn't included him in the death toll.

"Look at him, Doc. That'll be you, if you give the wrong answer."

Blake had been avoiding looking in that direction. Pictures were one thing. An actual corpse was quite another. The orderly was curled in the corner, his back facing Blake, a sagging brown stain across the seat of the white pants. Blake said, "Why won't you use his name, Teddy? He had a name."

"I know his name. It's Bob. I know all the guards." Teddy picked up the shank and the tape recorder. "Don't try that psycho stuff on me."

"You don't need those."

"I know. I could kill you with my hands." Teddy's speech was noticeably faster and more animated. He pressed stop on the recorder and set it back on the desk.

Blake needed to keep him calm and talking. "Why Bob? He was a nice guy. What did he do to you?"

"Nothing. Nothing at all. Far as I could tell, he was a swell guy."

"So why this?"

"Well, for one, I don't think he would exactly stand by and let this session go like this."

"No, I don't suppose he would have."

"But the real reason was he didn't answer the question correctly. I asked him last night when he locked me down."

"What'd he tell you?"

"C'mon, Doc. Don't cheat. If I tell you what he said, you'll know not to say it. I wouldn't want to give you any unfair advantages."

Strange. Teddy suddenly sounded more intelligent, but Blake figured he must be delirious from a loss of blood. "I thought you said I was smart. Surely I must be smarter than Bob."

"Damn, you're colder than I thought. This dude hasn't even been dead for ten minutes and you're already tearing apart his character."

Blake sat up, tried to block out his light-headedness and focus on Teddy. Maybe he was disoriented, but he could have sworn there was a twinkle in Teddy's piercing blue eyes that had never been there before. "I just meant that typically doctors are smarter than orderlies."

"I don't think that is necessarily true, but let's go ahead and say that it is. If you're so smart, tell me what Bob said."

"How could I possibly know that?"

"You tell me, Doc. Let's see those intellectual powers at work. There you go. You got smoke pouring out your ears. Don't worry, I was only speaking figuratively," he said, winking at the doctor. "Really got those gears in overdrive."

"It could've been anything. I don't know."

Teddy plunged the shank deep into Blake's thigh.

Blake clutched Teddy's fist and held it so the bastard couldn't pull it out. "Goddamn it, Teddy! Stop! Please."

Teddy twisted his fist. "Hurry up and tell me what Bob gave as his answer."

Blake gritted his teeth and held on as tight as he could. "I don't know! I mean I can't possibly be sure, but I know he didn't say it was anything to do with blood or his throat."

"True. I guess I can't expect anymore of you than that." Teddy shook his fist, the jagged metal tearing away at Blake's muscle. "But if you had to take a wild guess, what would you say?"

"Please stop! I can't think anymore. You can't kill me, Teddy. Do you know what number I would be?"

"Including the ones I got away with or just those you know about?"

Blake was silent a moment. "The ones we know?"

"I just said that Bob was ten." Teddy grinned. "Don't you know what comes after ten?"

"I know what it is, but I want to hear you say it."

"Eleven." Teddy ripped his hand backward, breaking Blake's grip and escaping with his knife. "How's that?"

"I have a wife, Teddy. Her name is Susanne."

Stop your sniffling and take a guess. I'd hurry if I were you. I'm starting to get bored. I kinda feel like painting."

A small volcano spewed lava where the shank had been. He stuffed part of his pants into the gushing wound. "You think they'll just let you go back to your room and daily activities after this?"

"Why not? What happened today isn't any different from what happened in the real world. I'm just a mentally challenged, confused young man trying to find the answer to a simple question."

"It's obvious you were faking that."

"Funny how it took you up until now to figure it out if it was so obvious."

"You're a good actor. We underestimated you."

"I know."

"They'll put you in prison. You'll be executed when they discover you were faking."

"How? The tape recorder is off. Bob's not telling them." Teddy nudged the orderly with his shoe. "Are you, Bob? No, I didn't think so. And I really doubt you'll tell them. You wouldn't break that patient/doctor confidentiality clause would you?"

"I wouldn't think of it."

"Nice try, you weasel. That doesn't protect me and we both know it. But enough stalling. What was Bob's answer? Three, two, one."

"Had you heard it before? Was it like any of the other answers?"

"For someone who's supposed to be answering a question, you seem to have a whole lot."

"Give me a chance."

"Fine, Doc. I'll give you a shot. It was similar to one of the answers I'd heard before, but I won't tell you whose."

"Bob was a pretty literal, straight forward kind of guy. I'm going to say he answered like your granddad's nurse. He either said the heart or brain."

"Wow, you are pretty smart. He said it was the brain. When a person is brain dead, in every sense of the word they're dead." Teddy held the jagged point to Blake's throat. "So tell me the answer. This really is your last chance."

Blake was too weak to fight. He couldn't even raise his hand above his stomach. "You must understand there is no true answer."

"Maybe you're right. Maybe there isn't. Everyone else said they knew, but they were all wrong. I proved that they were wrong. I got in trouble for it. That's not right. Getting in trouble because they were wrong."

"You got in trouble for committing nine acts of cold-blooded murder. Not for proving someone wrong."

"Guess it's a matter of opinion. So what makes you tick, Doc?"

"Personally? What motivates me? Is that what you're asking?"

"Sure."

"Teddy, is that what you're asking or not?"

"Don't worry. You can tell me."

"First, tell me why you did all this. Why pretend you were disabled? Your file said you've been slow ever since first grade."

Teddy shared his sick grin, applied more pressure with the shank. "You have any idea just how much you can get away with if people think you're even slightly retarded? And I'm not talking about this murder stuff. I'm talking day-to-day shit.

"You don't have to do schoolwork. You can ignore anyone you want. You can act any way you want. You can flip off your teacher and harass your schoolmates, and people write it off as you not knowing any better. It's the truest form of a free pass. Do what you want, when you want, to whoever you want, with almost no repercussions."

"And the stigma? You don't have a problem with that?"

"Who cares? Look what I did and look where I'm at. I get three meals, a ton of snacks, a nice cocktail of pills, all the painting materials I could ever want, and a bunch of retards to take advantage of. This place beats the real world any day."

"Why risk it then? Why'd you tell me?"

"I'm not risking anything? I just want your arrogant ass to realize there are smarter people out there than you. And I'm only 15."

"You should be proud of yourself," Blake said sarcastically.

"I am, but it doesn't sound like you are."

No one was coming to his rescue and Teddy was going to kill him. Blake had barely felt the blade break the skin, but his entire front was warm from the blood pouring down his chest. It wasn't so bad. It didn't hurt. It felt like he was sitting in a warm bath. If it weren't for Teddy's ice-cold, calculating smirk, this wouldn't be a bad way to go. He only hoped the others didn't fall for Teddy's low IQ act.

No Service

Shit. It'd been right in front of our faces and we hadn't seen it. The little girl's father had seemed so heartbroken, so devastated by her death. And the son of a bitch thinks he's going to get away with it.

There's only dark fields on both sides of the highway, nowhere to pull over to make the call. I punch in Dominic's number as I continue to drive and hit Send. The call fails. I try the department, another fail.

No bars at all. I probably won't have any service until the interstate. I don't want to wait that long, but I'm not turning around. As tempting as it is to drive back two hours and lead the arrest, I need to see Gabby before she hands me back the ring.

A sign reminds me there's a convenience store at the next exit. The store's open and I pull into the first of the three vacant parking spots. Still nothing on my phone to indicate service, so I get out and lock the car, head through the sliding doors.

The 20-something white guy sitting behind the counter doesn't even look up when the bell announces me. I walk to the counter, glad this isn't the same asshole clerk I had last time.

I count to five and he's still leaning back in his swivel chair, buried in a hunting magazine. I say, "Excuse me."

The clerk sets the magazine on his lap but doesn't say a word, the hate clear on his face. The look of contempt, like I'm a lower form of life, is one I learned to recognize as a kid. His name tag reads Erick, as if his parents couldn't decide which consonant they preferred.

"I'm sorry to bother you, but I need to borrow your phone."

He laughs. "Borrow my phone?"

I hold up my cell. "Yeah, I don't get any service out here."

"No one does."

"It's very important."

"I'm sure it is." Erick flips open his magazine. "Pay phone's right outside those doors."

"I need to call the police station."

"Like I said, the phone's outside."

I hate playing the cop card and want as few people as possible knowing what I do, but he's forcing my hand. "This is official police business."

"The phone here doesn't work. Been busted for a week."

"Why didn't you say that first?"

"You didn't ask."

This guy's worse than the first clerk, another racist like all the others that live out here. I'm tempted to check the phone, but I know he'll fight me. I walk back to my car and check the middle console for change, only able to scrounge up 35 cents. An older Pontiac pulls up with a portly blond and her little boy. I take a dollar bill from my wallet and follow them inside.

Erick has his feet propped up by the cash register, the phone held to his ear.

I say, "Excuse me."

He sighs into the receiver. "Hold on a sec." Looking at me like I stepped in shit, he says, "What now?"

"I thought the phone didn't work."

"Only incoming calls."

"I didn't hear it ring."

"You have superhuman hearing?"

I push the dollar across the counter. "Just break this for me and I'll be out of your hair."

Erick goes back to his telephone conversation. "Sorry 'bout that. You know some people. Always wanting something they can't have."

I slam my fist on the counter but keep my voice level. "I asked for change."

"And I assumed you could read." He points at the small poster board taped to the front of the cash register. "It says no change. You'll have to buy something."

I take a deep breath and unkink my neck, move it side to side. I can't let this fucker get to me.

I nearly bump into the blond on my way to the candy aisle. She asks Erick for quarters and he hands them over.

"What the hell is that? You just said I had to buy something to get change."

"You do."

"You gave her quarters." I hold the edge of the counter so I don't grab his throat.

"Her kid's gonna play the machine." He points to the videogame in the far corner. "That's pretty much buying something."

"And using the payphone isn't?"

"That's outside the store."

"I'm going to file a formal complaint."

"Am I supposed to be worried?"

I point at the camera peering down at us. "I want a copy of that footage."

"Can't have one."

"As a law enforcement officer, I'm demanding one."

"Well, as an employee of this store, I'm telling you you can't have one."

I lower my voice so the lady and her kid can't hear. "Listen up, you little asshole. I didn't come in here to cause trouble but that seems to be all that you care about. I want that tape."

Erick backs up and pulls a loose cable out of the wall. "See. It's not even hooked up to anything. The owner, who just happens to be my dad, got tired of buying tapes, and having to fix it. Plus, he said there's no point in having it since the cops never catch the fucking monkeys who rob us anyway." With a huge gap-toothed grin, he says, "Maybe you'd like to call him and complain about my unethical treatment."

"Just give me some change and I'll leave."

"Listen, I reserve the right to serve whoever I want, so while I'm still feeling generous, why don't you go buy something if you want that change? Now if you'll excuse me, I have a paying customer behind you."

The lady's smirk says she's enjoying this almost as much as he is. I ignore her and head down the far aisle, too angry to choose from the crackers, chips, and other crap. I take several deep breaths and unclench my hands, listen to the lady giggle.

My mother taught me a long time ago that being teased only hurts if you let it. I'd grown desensitized to it as a child, but taking it from some moron making ten bucks an hour is hard to swallow. Still, like Momma said, unless they lay a hand on you, don't pay them any mind.

The Pontiac pulls out of the parking lot. Erick punches numbers on the telephone that doesn't work, and I stand here like a child waiting for him to make me empty my pockets and accuse me of shoplifting.

I pick out a can of Pringles, a stick of jerky, and a bag of mixed nuts. I do the math and am looking for a 20-cent item when the sliding doors swoosh open. Shoes slap the tile, someone in a hurry.

A man shouts, "Hang up! Now!"

The phone clunks onto the receiver. I can't see but guess Erick's dad decided to check on the store.

The man says, "If you so much as move a goddamn inch, I'll blow your head off."

A deeper voice says, "Good. Now get face down on the floor. I'm coming over the counter. If you move, you die. Understand?"

The robbers must realize there's an extra car in the parking lot. I reach under my coat and ease out my service revolver as I crouch down. I only have six bullets and no reload. Not an ideal situation.

I creep to the edge of the aisle and watch one of the robbers, clad in black from shoes to ski mask, hop over the counter and open the register. He says, "A hundred and twenty dollars! Are you kidding me? Where's all the money?"

Erick tells him the night shift doesn't bring in much. There's a loud thud and Erick groans. "That's all we got," he says. "I got a 20 in my wallet. Take it. It's in my pocket."

The robber with the deep voice says, "Hey, man. Chill on the kicking."

"I ain't risking getting locked up again for a hundred bucks. Where's the safe? I know you got a one."

"We don't. You can go look. The office is open. We don't got one."

"Don't lie to me or I swear to God, I'll pull the trigger."

My thighs are on fire from crouching, but I stay still. I wish I knew where the second guy is but have to assume he's watching the door.

Erick is starting to sound like he's hyperventilating. "Look! Look in there! There's no safe. Take whatever you want, but there's no safe."

"Come on, man," the second guy says. "Grab the cash and some of those bottles and let's go."

"We need more than that." He asks Erick, "What about your car? Where're your keys?"

"I don't got one. My dad and I switch off at the shift exchange. I always use his."

"Don't lie to me. Give me your keys."

"I don't have any," Erick whines. "Check me."

"Then whose car is that if it ain't yours?"

I ease around the corner. The second robber is only an aisle away, back to me, his .45 pointed at the ground.

The one behind the counter is looking down. "I asked you a fucking question. Whose car?"

Erick says, "The dude is…" but I'm already moving. The second guy starts to turn but I crack his head with the butt of my .357. He crumbles and I turn the gun on the guy who just ducked beneath the counter.

I step back into a shooting stance, control my breathing, my gun sights steady. "I'm a cop. Raise your gun into the air by its barrel and come up very slowly."

"Fuck you. Johnny, you out there?"

"Out cold. Just you and me. I don't want any problems. Just give it up and no one else gets hurt."

Everything was silent except for the swishing of the Slurpee machine and my pounding heart. "What's it going to be? Do you really want to risk everything?"

"Back off or I'll put one through this dude's head."

"Let him go and we can talk about getting you out of here."

"Last warning. You better not fucking shoot," the robber says as he pops up using Erick as a shield.

Erick's pale and shaking, the robber behind him, the muzzle of the gun pressed to Erick's temple.

"You want to go away for murder?" I ask.

"I ain't going back, period. Walk out of here and this dude might live."

I steady my aim. "If you shoot him, I shoot you. Simple as that. You want to die?"

"Don't shoot me," Erick begs the robber. "Please don't shoot me. Don't listen to him." He tells me, "Just leave. Take off and let them go."

"Not an option."

The robber says, "Listen to him and leave."

"You know what, I don't give a rat's ass if you shoot him."

"Huh?" The robber looks like he's not sure he should believe me.

Erick says, "He's trying to psych you out. Just leave, cop. Come on. I'm sorry about earlier."

"Sure you are."

The robber says, "I'm gonna count to ten."

"Why so high? I've made my decision. It's you or me, and I'm going to see my girl tonight. Stop wasting my time and make your move."

Erick's tears are flowing. "Oh, man. Please don't do this. I just want to go home."

I say, "Now look what you did. You made him cry."

The robber remains silent.

I tell him, "Put your gun down and let's end this."

He hesitates a few seconds then sighs. "I'm gonna put the gun on the counter. Don't shoot."

"Good," I say as he complies. "Now take two steps to your left. That's good."

Erick moves to the right and I order him to stay put.

"I can't move?"

"Not yet. Let me handle this. Stay put."

Under his breath, he mutters, "You're all the same."

"What'd you say?"

"Nothing."

"No, you said something."

"Nothing. Just hurry up and arrest these two."

"Tell me what you meant."

"What you think I mean?"

The robber by my feet groans and brings his hands to the top of his head. I nudge him with my foot and say, "Johnny. Walk over to your partner."

Johnny squints up at me. "You a cop?"

"Get your ass over there."

Johnny is smart and does what he's told, blood dribbling down the pale skin on the exposed back of his neck.

Erick says, "Can I move now or what? Do I need to call some real cops?"

"How are you gonna call them? I thought the phone was busted."

"I thought you were in a big rush to go see your girl. I bet she's white, ain't she?"

I can't believe this prick has already forgotten that I was just saving his sorry ass. "What would you do if I walked out of here right now?"

"Pick up this gun, shoot these two, and report your black ass."

"Why would you shoot them? They're unarmed."

"There'd be two less of your kind to go around and rob someone else."

I tell the robbers to take off their masks.

Both robbers are as white as Erick, looking like raccoons with the dark makeup spread around their eyes and lips.

"My kind?" I look at the clock and say, "It is getting late and I do want to see my fiancée, who, by the way, is just as dark as I am. Let's wrap this up." I turn to the first robber. "You'll be going back to prison for this, right?"

"At least 10, probably 20," he says, sounding broken.

"More depending on how I write it." I take the gun off the counter, back up a few steps and set it down. "And you don't want to go back?"

"God, no!"

"Well, as you and Johnny can imagine, I'm pretty tired of this idiot…"

"What the hell are you doing?" Erick says, "Why're you talking to them?"

I ignore him. "That security camera doesn't work. The nearest police substation is over a half-hour away, and they never send cars out here. If I walk out of here, you never saw me."

Everyone's stunned. Johnny asks, "You're gonna let us go?"

Erick shouts, "It's not funny. Arrest them!"

"One condition. He didn't see me either."

When the realization of what I just said kicks in, Johnny says, "Hold on. I didn't come in here to do that."

"Did you come in to get locked up for armed robbery and attempted murder of a police officer?" I take another step and the sliding doors swoosh open. I look at his partner and say, "You on board? He never saw me."

The first robber nods.

I turn my back on them, the doors muffling Erick's screams. I can barely hear him when I climb inside the car, not at all with the music on.

I'm back on the road, my breathing normal. Sometimes you have to do the wrong thing for the right reasons. Sometimes reason doesn't play a part and emotions take over. Either way, it's time to move on. I pull out my phone. Maybe now I'll get some service.

In Charge

The speed limit's 65, my cruise control set to 63, the right lane all mine. Sunday nights are always slow, but this is getting ridiculous, only 22 cars passing in the last half-hour, 14 with men in them.

That's barely one out of three, Fred says smugly.

There's no one around to see me talking to an empty car so I say, "Thanks, Fred, but I can do the math."

Yeah, thanks, you fucking dork, Tommy says.

"Knock it off, Tommy. This ain't the time or place," I say real serious so he knows I'm not messing around.

Oooooh, Tommy says. *I'm so scared.*

Fred asks, *How about we listen to the radio?*

I say, "Good idea," and push it on.

Tommy says, *How about you stop being such a little bitch?*

I don't know if he means me or Fred, but either way it doesn't matter. We all know I can silence them if I want to. The pink pills in the bathroom provide a viable solution.

Tommy laughs. *Holy shit. Viable? You fucking hear yourself?*

I turn up the Mozart, not about to engage with the dickhead.

The song ends and headlights pop up in the rearview.

Drop it down, Tommy tells me.

"No shit," I say. "This ain't my first time."

Oh, I remember that, Fred sighs.

How the fuck I get stuck with you two? Tommy asks.

I'm going 61 as the headlights switch to the outside lane. They're too low to be an SUV, and I sense my odds dropping.

Relax, Fred says. *Stay cool.*

The car's a Toyota, some wrinkly fucker with a gray goatee bobbing his head to a beat.

This is some bullshit, Tommy says.

I set the cruise control back to 63, let the guy disappear down the interstate. "Maybe it's time to turn around."

What? It's not even nine," Tommy says like I can't read the clock.

I turn off the radio because it's too much stimulation and I'm getting agitated. "Ever think maybe we'll have better luck eastbound?"

Figure'd you were just bitching out, worried about waking up for work.

"Getting up at six ain't easy."

You don't think we know that?

Fred tells Tommy to drop it. *Charles is getting upset.*

Sorry, Charlie.

I pass Exit 21, spot a minivan merging onto the interstate just ahead. I catch up but keep my distance, stay close enough to see her Pennsylvania plates, the sticker family on the back window.

We may be in luck, Fred says.

Only one way to find out.

I keep quiet, speed up to match the van, but can't tell who's driving. Knowing Tommy won't keep quiet, I flip on my signal and switch lanes. I'm even with the back of the van when I spot the driver in the van's side mirror, a fat 50-something face with too much makeup.

So? Tommy practically shouts. *The ugly ones love it the most.*

I can't argue with that and ease off the gas, fall in behind her.

Shit! Tommy says. *Passenger seat.*

There's the brim of a baseball hat, someone's shoulder sticking out.

Could be another woman.

I drop the LeSabre to 63. "Really, Fred? I'm disappointed. Stick to the rules so there's no problems. Two's a crowd no matter their sex."

Mmmmmm, Pablo says like the word's delicious. *Sex.*

"No, no, no," I tell him. "You're not needed yet."

Andale, puto.

"We're turning back next exit if I hear another word."

Headlights appear in the rearview, the vehicle catching up.

Oh shit, Tommy says when we see it's a big boxy van. *Maybe she's a handy.*

"That was one time," I say, not proud I accidentally pulled out the woman's colostomy bag.

But, ay yi yi, that was hot.

I tell Pablo, "You're not helping."

Oh yeah, Pappi? Then why's your cock out?

I stuff it back in my sweats. "Had an itch."

The van passes on my left, a tough guy with dreads behind the wheel.

Before I get too upset, another car flies up from behind, its headlights enough to make the van move over.

Hot tamale on its way, Pablo says.

I take it to 69 and Pablo moans. I tell him, "Grow up."

The car flies by, the cute blond a blur.

After her, Tommy says.

My dick's still hard, throbbing at the thought, but, just like the voices, I can't let it control me. "You got money to pay for the ticket?"

Or a trip to jail? Fred asks.

When did you become such a fucking pussy?

Exit 23 is a half-mile ahead. Time to turn back.

Come on, Tommy says. *You want this just as much as us.*

"What I want is for you to shut your mouth so I can concentrate on the road."

Tommy laughs. *And grab your dick.*

"I had an itch!"

Yeah, a little one, Tommy says real low so I can barely hear him.

Headlights appear way back but they won't reach me before the exit.

Don't do it, Tommy says. *I was fucking around. We all know you have the juiciest hog.*

He knows how much I hate sarcasm. "I'll fucking show you."

Woah, I'm no fag, Charlie.

"I'm taking the pills when we get home. There might be three of you, but never forget, I'm the motherfucker in charge."

Oh my, a delicate female voice says.

"Pablo?"

Wasn't me, Papi.

The van's gone, the headlights about seven car lengths back.

"Tommy?"

Do I sound like a bitch?

115

I got both hands on the wheel, a sick feeling in my gut. "What's your name?"

The woman of your dreams, she says all smooth and silky, sexiest voice I've ever heard.

Charles, Fred says, *you need to tell us something?*

He's going to transition, Tommy says with his asshole laugh.

I know it sounds ridiculous, but I shout, "I'm not a woman!"

Oh, I know that, she says. *I'm not in your head, baby.*

A black BMW 745i pulls alongside, limousine tinted windows.

Tommy says, *Bet it's a hundred-pound hipster with a hair bun.*

The passenger window rolls down, revealing a beautiful 40-ish woman with long jet-black hair staring straight ahead.

Oh my fucking God, Tommy says. *You guys see this?*

I keep my lips close together so she doesn't think I'm talking to myself. "Play it cool."

Rich women have rich husbands at home, Fred says, *not to mention top-of-the-line security systems.*

Tommy says, *The higher the risk, the higher the reward.*

Fred says, *Too good to be true means she's a cop. You know police are searching for us. Probably people in the backseat.*

Out of my three voices, Fred's the one who's usually right. I ease off the gas and let the BMW pull ahead. "Yeah, too risky," I say because Tommy's going nuts.

The BMW puts on its blinker and moves into my lane, matches my speed. *You don't get it*, she says. *With me, there is no risk.*

I keep my mouth shut in case she's watching me in her rearview, but Tommy and Pablo are losing their minds.

The blinker clicks on again and I say, "Okay, everyone keep it down. She's getting off. Should I —"

Tommy shouts, *Yes!*

There's only a right turn at the bottom of the exit ramp, a dead end to the left. The road's barely wide enough for one car in each direction, and in the dark it's easy to see no one's coming. I've never been out here, but love the isolation, nothing but trees and bushes, bushes and trees.

Maybe you should slow down, Fred says. *Don't want to scare her.*

I'm letting off the gas when Tommy says, *You serious? This is like an act of God. For some crazy reason this hot chick wants to take you to Bone Town.*

Fred says he's never heard of it. Pablo chuckles.

There's about five car lengths between us, just enough space to keep Fred quiet.

The moon disappears and our world is the circle of headlights, huge pines blocking us in on both sides. The cloud blows by and it's a little less creepy, a state park sign pointing to the right.

The BMW's blinker pops on, tick, tick, tick. We're down to 10 miles an hour when she pulls into the deserted parking lot.

Parks close after dark, Fred says.

Really, dude? You're a full-blown fucktard, Tommy says like it's a fact. *Someone bought her that car and she doesn't want him finding out. Simple as that.*

She parks in the farthest stall, the one closest to the forest.

What if she's a dude? Fred asks, real quiet.

It takes Tommy a second. *Well, then that motherfucker's pretty hot.*

I park in front of the bathrooms, about 10 stalls between us.

Tommy says, *Don't be such a chicken shit.*

"I don't want to scare her."

Well, then maybe you should stop talking to us, Tommy says. *Look, there she goes.*

Pablo sighs. *O Dios mío.* The BMW's headlights illuminate her incredible body, a short leather skirt hugging her hips as she heads down the dirt path.

I pop the glovebox, stuff the blackjack into my back pocket. Fred usually tells me not to, but this time it's Tommy. He says, *Why ruin the fun?*

The BMW's headlights click off, everything dark when I shut off the engine and open my door. There's a small sliver of moon poking through the clouds, but I can't see the woman.

The night is silent except for my shoes squishing on the spongy grass. I get on the path and follow it toward the opening in the trees.

The clearing is empty except for the woman standing in the middle, the moonlight caressing her angelic face. She waves me forward, her bright red lips motionless when she says in that same sexy voice, *Don't be afraid. I want you in me.*

I've never once heard those words and worry I won't be able to perform without the thrill of the hunt.

Pablo says, *You got this.*

Tommy says, *Knock her upside the head if things go south.*

It feels like a dream as I glide toward her, stop a few feet away. *The perfect distance if you need to bonk her,* Fred says.

Her fingers pop one, two, three buttons of her black blouse. She holds out her hands. "Don't you want me?" she asks out loud in the same voice. "Don't you want to be in me?"

I lick my lips, calm myself with my hand on the blackjack.

She unbuttons the last two, no bra underneath. "Do you want to be inside me?"

I know my voice will shake, but I say, "You know I do."

"Then come here, Charles."

I leave the blackjack in my pocket and step into her warm embrace. "Did you say my name?"

Her hand lands on my crotch and squeezes. "Does it matter?"

I grunt no.

She releases me and steps out of the moonlight, her soft skin sloughing off, the dead skin underneath cracked and peeling.

I've never had visual hallucinations, but I pray that's what's happening. My voices are gone, and it's just me and this monster.

Her almond-shaped eyes narrow to slits, her black iris's flashing bright red. Her lips peel back from her gigantic maw filled with dozens of razor-sharp teeth.

I squeeze my eyes shut, hope the vision will disappear. I open them and she's back in the moonlight just inches away, leaning in for a kiss, a monstrous vision no more. I give her a quick peck on her cheek and say, "I'm sorry. I just had a moment. Not feeling too well."

"You feel just fine to me," she says, reminding me with a squeeze.

I look away from her moonlit face, horrified to see her cracked claw. She flexes her forearm, the talons punching through my sweats and testicles.

119

The hand on my chest pushes and I fall flat on my back, my manhood shredded. The beast leans over me, shows her true self as she leaves the moonlight. "Oh, Charles, it's going to be so much fun."

I scramble back, but she pins me down with her foot, shakes her head.

Slobber oozes out of the corners of her mouth and lands on my chest, burns through my shirt and skin. "I do want you in me. All of you." She unhinges her jaw and shows me there's no body part too big for her. "Give it to me, baby."

Marked

Olsen was too good to be true. The old man hadn't learned his lesson. He still flaunted his wealth, kept the same exact routines, and never watched his back. It was like the fat slob wanted to get robbed again.

When Nick first got out of the joint, he'd promised himself he'd never do this sort of thing again, but Olsen was the perfect victim and the money was too good. Three hundred thousand would solve a lot of problems. It'd also make up a little for the time locked up. Hell, a payday like that would equal close to fifty thousand for each of his seven years in the pen.

Nick turned the page of the newspaper and sneaked another glance at the jewelry store directly across from the mall's food court. From his seat outside of the McDonald's Express, he could keep a close eye on the old man while looking like any other fool reading the help wanted ads. Not that he would ever lower himself to take one of those jobs. Just for the hell of it, he ran through the list. The only positions he qualified for were below him. And the other 90 percent of the jobs wouldn't be worth taking, even if the manager had no hang-up about hiring an uneducated ex-con. Who wants to wear a monkey suit and take orders from some college dork just to make thirty thousand a year? To hell with that.

It was nearing seven o'clock and Suzanne, his inside, was pleasantly escorting the last couple out of the jewelry store. Before she headed back in, Suzanne made eye contact with Nick and gave him a discrete thumbs up. He set down his paper to acknowledge her, and she flashed four fingers. This was going to be sweeter than he had imagined. Olsen was taking home more work than usual.

Nick grabbed his coffee and headed for the exit. Olsen wouldn't be done closing up shop for another half hour, but Nick was too excited to stay still. Four hundred thousand. A hundred thousand for each of the months he'd been out on parole, unable to find a decent job.

Olsen's car wasn't in its spot. The black BMW had been there when Nick arrived two hours before and it should still be there. Olsen hadn't left his sight for more than five minutes. No way he could have come out and moved it.

Nick was tempted to race back inside to find Suzanne, but that would be foolish. It wouldn't look good for a tattooed thug to be seen with her. Someone might get the wrong idea and put things together, especially if he went ahead with the robbery. He couldn't bring her into it. Not because he liked her, but because he didn't trust her. Just like everyone else on the planet, if it was her ass or his, she would sell him out in a second. Just like the backstabbing bastard that had put him away in the first place.

Not sure what to do, Nick did a 180 and headed for his beater Ford. He felt like a fool when he spotted Olsen's 745i in the next row, wedged between two SUVs. He had to get a grip if he was going to pull this thing off. How could he not know where the car was parked? He was acting like a damn fish straight out of the tank.

Easing into his lowered front seat, Nick concentrated on the BMW's driver door, rationalizing away his fear. He had nothing to worry about. Olsen was an easy target. He'd been an easy target for Bear and hadn't changed his ways since.

Bear, now that was an untrustworthy son of a bitch. After sharing a six-by-eight concrete cell for two years, you'd think you'd get to know someone. They'd sworn allegiance to each other, become blood brothers, beaten down punks together. All that, and Bear still ditched him when it counted. Three months ago, Bear had called Nick to tell him about this mark. They were supposed to do it together and split the profit, but Bear must've got greedy because, after a week of staking out and planning with Nick, he went ahead and did it on his own.

The only decent thing Bear did was give Suzanne Nick's name and number so she could call him a week later and tell him that Bear had taken her boss for close to two hundred thousand. The good news was that the plan had worked and the old man continued his reckless ways. The bad news was Bear split town without saying a word, which seemed pretty risky considering he was on paper for the next three years. Probably went to Mexico where he wouldn't have to worry about some parole officer making house calls.

Nick knew all about that headache. As far as pigs went, his PO was pretty cool, but the guy was still a pain in the ass. He held Nick's parole papers over his head, constantly reminding him that the smallest screw-up would send him back in to finish his last two years. And the home invasion he had planned would earn him more than a slap on the wrist; most likely an additional five-to-ten on top of the two. The one thing Nick knew was he would never go back.

He considered calling the whole thing off. Maybe it wasn't worth the risk. Nick had missed the first seven years of his only son's childhood, precious years he would never get back. In the past four months he'd seen glimpses of the father he could be if he only stayed out of prison. How could he risk missing another seven? Nicky deserved better than that. Then again, getting a crappy, minimum-wage job wasn't much of an option either. What kind of role model would he be if he could barely afford to take his son out for a Happy Meal? He needed money and he needed it now. He would just have to be extra careful.

The dashboard clock read 7:40. Olsen was already ten minutes late. Instead of getting worked up about the delay, Nick counted his blessings. The sun had set, and it would be difficult for the old man to spot him.

Nick didn't have to wait much longer. Without checking his surroundings, Olsen unlocked his Beemer and slid his leather overcoat across the backseat. After stroking his bushy, gray goatee, he plopped into the driver's seat, tossing his briefcase onto the passenger side.

Just the sight of the treasured briefcase made Nick's imagination run wild. There was no question whether or not he would do this; the man was an easy target with a huge payoff. What more could he ask for?

Not worried if he lost Olsen for a moment or two, Nick gave him a few seconds head start. He knew the route Olsen would take and that he wouldn't deviate from it. All that mattered was that Nick arrived at the house just before the fat man pulled in.

Nick was stopped three cars behind Olsen's when they reached the traffic signal marking the halfway point. After slipping on his black leather gloves, Nick checked the glovebox and pulled out his gun. The .38 wasn't in the best condition, and possession of it would land him back in the pen, but the reassuring feel of the hard metal gave him the confidence he needed right now. For this kind of job he should really have a partner, but he couldn't risk trusting anyone. He'd made that mistake with Bear, and he wasn't going to make it again. And if that idiot had been able to do this on his own, then there was no reason Nick couldn't pull it off.

As expected, Olsen drove two blocks down and pulled into the McDonald's drive-thru. Nick knew the slob would order three Big Macs, two large fries, a large strawberry shake, an apple pie, and a caramel sundae. And judging by the cars ahead of Olsen, it would take six to eight minutes for him to get his food and reenter traffic. Plenty of time for Nick to get to the house.

Olsen's sparsely populated neighborhood was beautiful, the type of place Nick could never afford. He hoped he wouldn't have to use the gun. He didn't want to hurt, let alone kill, anyone. It wasn't his style, but prison had taught him an important lesson in life: sometimes you have to be violent to survive. If it came down to him or Olsen, he wouldn't hesitate to pull the trigger.

The original plan had called for Bear to hide in the garage and have Nick tail the Beemer. Once it pulled into the garage, Nick would block Olsen in. Now that he was flying solo, he would have to improvise.

If he tried driving in behind the Beemer, Olsen would be sure to spot him and could easily close the garage door before Nick could slip inside. If Nick hid in the garage, he'd have to worry about Olsen driving away if he smelled something fishy. And that was if he could even get inside the garage. Suzanne said the code still worked, but who knew how accurate that info was.

Nick pulled onto Olsen's street, passed the house, made a U-turn, and parked directly across from the driveway that divided the eight-foot-high wall surrounding the property. With about five minutes left to get into position, Nick tucked the pistol into the waistband of his jeans and eased out of the car. Acting as if he had business being there, he sauntered across the street and entered Olsen's lushly landscaped property. The house was to his right, and directly before him was the attached three-car garage. He slid open the small remote on the wall and punched in Suzanne's code, praying it would work. The door rumbled open and before it had risen halfway, Nick had already slipped inside, knocked loose the automatic light, and hit the switch that lowered the door.

Nick crouched in the corner and waited for his eyes to adjust to the darkness. When he heard a car pull into the driveway, Nick backed against the side wall and ducked behind some barrels. He remembered to slip on his black ski mask just as the garage door began to rise.

The piercing headlights illuminated the garage, allowing Nick to see he was hiding behind two plastic trash cans. Nick peered through the crack between the cans and saw the tail end of the BMW pulling in. He also noticed the electric gate sliding shut. In all the days he had staked out the house, with Bear and without him, he had never once seen the gate close. He hadn't even realized there was a gate, but thinking back he did remember walking across its track. Why Olsen decided to close it now was beyond him, but Nick guessed it was a good thing. Sure, he'd have to jump over it when he left, but this made the house much more secure and isolated from the outside. Now, he needn't worry about some Good Samaritan spotting him and calling the cops.

The car's engine and headlights turned off. Nick pulled out the .38 and gathered his nerves as the garage door closed. Now was the most important moment. No more hiding, no more waiting.

Olsen seemed to be taking a long time getting out of the car, and Nick wondered if he might be on his cell phone. If Olsen got out of the car and was still on the phone, Nick was screwed.

Five seconds ticked away before the car door creaked open. Nick strained his ears but couldn't hear anything. Although Olsen wasn't talking, he could be listening to someone on the phone. The fat man's dress shoes clicked onto the cold concrete and the door slammed shut. Still no talking. Nick had to act. If the old man was on the phone, he'd signal for him to turn it off. And if the guy tried something squirrelly, Nick would deal with him, snag that briefcase and run like hell.

Before Olsen took another step, Nick popped up. He had worried for nothing. The briefcase was in his hand, but no phone.

Nick aimed the gun at Olsen's head. "Hold it right there."

The guy didn't even flinch. He slowly turned to face Nick, the Beemer between them. Olsen was smiling.

"Hold it right there," Nick repeated.

"I heard you the first time."

If the car hadn't been in the way, Nick would have slapped the smug bastard. "Put the briefcase on the hood and slide it over."

"But the paint. Surely you wouldn't want me to scratch it."

"Are you serious? Put the goddamn briefcase on the car!"

"Calm down, son. You don't want to use that."

"I will."

"No, you won't."

"Yes, I will!"

A soft voice sounded from the opposite corner, startling Nick. "Not if you want to live."

Without taking the gun off Olsen, Nick glanced to his right. Dressed in black, barely recognizable in the dark, Suzanne crouched behind Olsen's other car, a pistol pointed at Nick's head.

Nick was so frustrated and upset he could barely speak. "What the hell are you doing?"

"What does it look like?"

"Put the gun down."

"Now why would she want to do that?" Olsen asked.

Nick turned his attention back to Olsen. His smile was maddening. "I'll shoot you."

"No you won't, Nicholas. You'll drop your gun and acknowledge that you made a very bad mistake coming here."

Nick turned his gun on Suzanne. Olsen whipped out a huge revolver and trained it on Nick.

Nick moved the gun from Olsen to Suzanne and back again. "What is this crap? You were helping me. What happened? Did he find out? Make you do this?"

"Are you really that stupid?" She stood and walked around the trunk of the Jag. "Not even Bear was that stupid. Now put down your gun."

"Do as she says. Shooting you will give me little pleasure. Not to mention it will make quite a mess, which I really have no interest in cleaning."

Nick couldn't speak, but he continued moving the gun from one target to the other.

"Really, Nick," Suzanne said, walking over to Olsen with her gun lowered. "Put it down. You really think I'd give you a working gun?"

When Bear had given it to Nick, he'd hidden it away, automatically assuming it functioned. He never once thought about trying it, and it wasn't as if he could take it to the firing range.

Nick continued to aim at Olsen. "I'll put mine down when he puts his down."

"Now that's not very smart, Nicholas."

"Quit calling me that, you fat bastard."

"That's not very nice. Set the gun down, and, while you're at it, why don't you take off your mask and get comfortable."

Suzanne switched on the garage's light and slid her slight frame against Olsen, a man twice her age and three times her weight.

"Okay, this is getting very tedious," Olsen said, switching guns with Suzanne. "If you insist on forcing me to shoot you, I'd better use this one."

Nick aimed at the side of Olsen's round head and pulled the trigger. He pulled it again. And again. Nothing.

"Now will you put it down?" Olsen raised the silenced pistol. "I really didn't invite you here just to shoot you."

Nick dropped the worthless gun and pulled off his mask, recognizing defeat. "Let me go. I didn't do anything. This is entrapment."

Suzanne smiled as she ran her hand over Olsen's belly. "We're not cops, so entrapment doesn't mean all that much to us. If you'd like to call the police and tell them about it, I'd be more than happy to let you use my phone." Suzanne held out her cell. "I'm sure they'd agree with you and lock us up. They wouldn't question why you were on another man's property without his permission. They also wouldn't wonder what an ex-felon is doing with a firearm."

Nick shook his head at the phone and asked them what they wanted.

"We merely desire your presence," Olsen said, "and we didn't think you'd accept our request."

"But why? What do you want?"

"To show you something. Come with us. Go ahead, Nicholas. Follow Suzanne."

With no option but to do as he was told, Nick trailed Suzanne through the laundry room and into the kitchen. He considered trying to grab her and use her as a shield, but he could feel Olsen's gun pressing against his back.

"You still haven't told me why." Nick watched Suzanne's hips switching back and forth as she led them down a long hallway. "I didn't do anything to you. I don't even know you?"

"Nicholas, my boy, you are really in no position to demand an explanation," Olsen said. "But I am feeling generous. The truth is that I'm a big reality TV buff. Problem is the quality of shows they give us." Olsen urged Nick into the room Suzanne had entered. "Go ahead."

From the looks of it, Olsen had his own little movie studio. Nick counted over 20 screens and a wall full of recording equipment in the room.

"The mindless programs they call entertainment are insulting to my intelligence. Shows about love, infatuation, infidelity, sex. Shows about cliques, pacts, alliances, betrayals. Garbage. All garbage."

Suzanne hit a switch that blanked out all the screens.

"So what's your brilliant idea?" Nick asked. "What do you have that Hollywood hasn't thought of?"

"A glimpse into man's true spirit."

"What do I have to do?"

"Spend the next three months in my guestroom." Olsen pointed at the metal door Suzanne stood next to.

"What's the catch?"

"There is none."

"And if I refuse?"

"What do you think the gun's for, Nicholas?"

Nick searched their faces for some clue. He knew there was more to the story, but he didn't really have an option. "Three months? And then you just let me go? No cops?"

"You have my word. Now if you would be so kind as to give Suzanne your car keys, we'll park your car in the garage so you don't get towed."

"How thoughtful." Nick threw his keys at Suzanne.

"Now, now, Nicholas. Be a sport."

Nick wouldn't look at him.

"That's fine. I've had enough of your uncivil company." Olsen motioned toward the door. "Go ahead, Suze."

The door swung open, revealing a long corridor with another metal door at the end of it. Nick walked the hallway, the door slamming shut behind him. When he came to the far end of the hallway, he said, "And how exactly am I supposed to get in?"

A loud click answered his question. Nick pushed the unlocked door open and stepped into the dark chamber. The second he was clear of the door, it slammed shut behind him, the lock snapping back into place.

Assuming the cameras were equipped with audio, Nick said, "So you're going to see if I'm scared of the dark. 'Fraid not, big guy. You'll have to do better than that."

The lights turned on, momentarily blinding him. Nick squinted and saw he was inside a rather large, but otherwise ordinary, guestroom. There was no dungeon master with whips and chains, no rabid dog, no bed of roaches. Just a large, windowless room with a cot against one wall, a couch across from it, and a toilet and sink in the far corner. If Olsen got his jollies watching grown men taking a crap on camera, then maybe this wasn't going to be as bad as Nick thought.

A low moan came from the couch. There was someone sitting there looking at him. The unclothed man rose to his feet, his emaciated body tottering on spindly legs.

Over a loudspeaker, Olsen said, "You're not being very polite, Nicholas. You could at least say hello."

"Didn't know I was getting a roommate."

"I thought you'd be happy. You haven't seen each other in quite some time."

This poor bastard with his protruding ribs and bloated stomach couldn't weigh more than a hundred pounds, surely no one Nick knew.

"True, he looks a little worse for wear, but that's no reason to ignore him."

The bearded man inched closer. He held something shiny in his hand. His bony right hand with the shamrock and swastika tattooed across it. The same exact tattoo Nick had spent hours working on between count times.

"I know Bear is happy to see you. He hasn't had a thing to eat in over — what is it? — seven days. And that doesn't include the 80 days prior in which he was given a mere thousand calories."

Eighty-seven days. A couple shy of Olsen's deadline. "Stop right there," Nick ordered his old cellmate.

Bear didn't stop. Only five feet separated them. He pointed the knife at Nick's chest.

"What's it going to be, fellows? Who's going to make it to see tomorrow? Bear, you win and you'll finally get to eat and in a few days have your freedom. Nicholas, if you're the victor, you'll have three months to wonder who your final meal will be. Have at it, boys. Tape is rolling."

Gone for Good

This was the exact reason Joanne left Los Angeles and moved halfway across the country to a small town. This type of savage atrocity was only supposed to be committed by the filthy creatures that inhabited large cities. Gruesome murders weren't supposed to happen out here in the middle of nowhere.

After one last look at the body, Joanne exited the bedroom and made her way toward Officer Donavan, who was pacing back and forth at the end of the hallway.

Joanne asked, "Were you the first to respond?"

Donavan said, "Yeah, Kenmore was on the other side of town helping Miss O'Connor with her chickens. I was picking up lunch at the diner when I heard the call. Sure am glad I hadn't eaten yet."

"It's not a pretty sight in there," she said, letting him know that if a seasoned veteran like herself was upset by it, then he had nothing to be embarrassed about.

"God, she was just a helpless old woman. And the number of times she was stabbed. It's sick."

Joanne shook her head. Someone the victim's age should be baking cookies for her grandkids or knitting a sweater. She had no business being spread across the bed, having spent her last few minutes on earth as a human pincushion.

"What can you tell me? Do we know anything yet?"

"Diana Snyder. Sixty-seven years old. No sign of forced entry. Guessing she left the door unlocked. Her husband, George, found her and called 911." He nodded toward the kitchen doorway behind him. "He's in there. When I came in, he was cuddled up beside her."

"How's he holding up?"

"He's stopped crying. I think he's in shock."

"Okay. I can take it from here."

"Care if I wait outside? I don't know if I can handle listening to him anymore. It's too damn sad."

"That's fine. Start interviewing the neighbors. They were probably too far away to see anything, but you never know."

Donavan hurried out the front door. Joanne walked toward the kitchen, took a deep breath, and braced herself. This had to be the absolute worst part of the job. She would rather examine a dozen mutilated bodies than interview one survivor, especially so soon after the incident.

The distraught man sat the small kitchen table, his once-white T-shirt splattered with blood. Joanne slowly crossed the linoleum floor, giving herself time to steady her nerves and study him.

The bony old man was a wreck, his wiry, white hair scattered every which way, streaked a dark-brownish red from having run his bloody hands through it. His blood-shot eyes were such a pale blue that it looked like the years had peeled away their brilliance. He had an average looking nose, straight and without bumps, but a strand of clear mucus hung between the tufts of white hair that pushed from each nostril.

Standing with her hand on the back of an empty chair, Joanne said, "Excuse me, Mr. Snyder."

The man looked at Joanne. "She's gone," he said, his voice cracked and desolate. "Gone for good."

Gently, she asked, "Do you mind if I sit down, sir?"

He clenched his hands. "Oh God. I can't believe it."

Joanne took a seat and offered him the package of tissues she kept in her jacket.

His large, round eyes overflowed with anguish. "It's George."

Joanne set the tissues on the table, hoping he would use them to wipe his nose. George continued talking, oblivious to the gesture and the dangling string of snot about to drop onto his upper lip.

"We were high school sweethearts, you know," he said, eyes fixed on his hands.

Joanne nodded. In her 16 years in the LAPD she had discovered that, if time permitted, it was best to let the survivors talk about other things before addressing the tragic event. It seemed to serve them as a type of security blanket that would lessen the impact of reliving the terrible trauma.

George said, "Ever since she took the seat in front of me in freshman English. I'd stare at her auburn mane and imagine caressing it. She was beautiful."

Joanne had never been loved by any one man for more than five years, but here was George idolizing a wife he'd had for 50.

"The first time she let me hold her hand, we were walking down Cherry Avenue, my arm burning from the weight of our school books. From that moment on I never let go."

Joanne was tempted to grab the tissues for herself. She couldn't let the tears flow, that would be unprofessional, even in this hick town. Joanne knew she should be asking questions in case the killer was fleeing the area, but she figured a few more minutes wouldn't hurt. Whoever had committed the atrocity had not been careful. They would have more than enough evidence to track down the animal.

"We got married 48 years ago and had three wonderful children. We made them on that same exact bed that she was…"

The old man looked at Joanne, really looked at her for the first time. "Why did this have to happen? It wasn't supposed to. We were going to die together."

Joanne cleared her throat. "I don't know. I'm so sorry."

"She's only been gone an hour but it feels like an eternity. I don't know how I'll ever make it without her."

"You will," she said.

"If only things had been different. I feel like it's my fault."

"Did you leave the door unlocked?"

"No, everything was locked, but this could have been prevented. She didn't heed my warnings."

Joanne imagined his unsuspecting wife opening the front door and inviting the killer inside to use the phone or perhaps the bathroom.

George said, "And what a terrible way to go. Must have taken over five minutes and she was alive most of it."

There were 77 slashes shredding Diana's body but only a few delivered to the torso. Joanne eased her chair back and asked, "Did you hear the attack?"

"Is she still on the bed?"

"George. Where were you this morning?"

He used the back of his hand to wipe his nose, dragging the slimy mucus across his cheek. "I was here all day."

"In the backyard?"

He shook his head. "I warned her to change. It didn't have to end this way."

The Season

Dylan looked out the side windows instead of concentrating on his driving. "Damn, ain't no one out here. Usually tons of fools running the street. And where all the whores at?"

"Got me, Dee." Brad shrugged, and then pointed to the garbage-strewn curb. "Park right there. Behind that heap."

Dylan turned off the struggling engine. "We shouldn't talk. I'm surprised this piece even made it here."

"Be happy Enrique let us borrow it. I ain't bringing my ride down here, and I know you weren't about to bring the Hummer."

"Hell no. It'd be up on blocks before we got out." Dylan checked the street one more time before unlocking the doors. "You ready?"

Brad stepped out into the dark night. "Smell that air. Nothing like the sweet ocean breeze rushing through Long Beach."

Dylan coughed. "Might smell decent if the Pacific wasn't as green as your shirt."

Brad went up the staircase that led to apartment 3B. "Come on, before someone sees us."

Dylan stopped halfway up. "Dude, this is kinda freaking me out. It ain't even nine and the streets are empty."

"Stop tripping, homie. Probably some party nearby. Free crack for everyone."

Brad knocked and flakes of brown paint floated to the porch.

A gruff voice barked, "Who's there?"

Dylan stepped back and whispered, "Is that T? Don't sound like him."

"It's us. Me and Dee. Let us in."

The door opened just enough for a silver-plated barrel to point out. "Let me see your hands."

Dylan said, "Come on, man. We're cool."

"Let me see your hands and then slowly turn around. Do it. Now."

They completed their spins and the door opened. The brawny black man waved them inside with his gun, shut the door behind them, and slid the deadbolt.

Dylan asked, "What's up with the new security procedures? You get jacked since last week?"

Brad nodded at the .45. "Yeah, put that thing away, bro. You know we're cool."

Tyrone eased the gun into the waistband of his jeans. "I don't trust anyone. Especially crazy ass white boys. That's how people get killed."

"Damn, it's like that," Brad said, pretending his feelings were hurt. "Well, I guess we should get down to business. You don't have a problem with white boys' money do you?"

"Never had a problem with that." Tyrone peeled back the front window's curtain. "What'd you guys ride in?"

"The primered Ford out front," Brad said.

"No wonder the cops didn't turn you around," Tyrone said, more to himself than his company. "You two have a seat while I get your stuff. Same amount?"

"Yeah, a quarter pound," Dylan said. "That should last us to next week."

"That's four grand. You cool with that?"

Dylan joined Brad on the couch. "We gotta see it first,"

"Sit tight and I'll be right back. Whatever you do, don't open that goddamn door."

Dylan waited for Tyrone to leave the room before he whispered, "What's up with your boy? Why's he all uptight?"

"First off, he isn't my boy," Brad said. "We're cool but that's it. Probably had a bad deal earlier. That's why he doesn't want us getting the door."

"I don't know; he's high-strung as hell. Don't need him waving that gun around when he's like this."

"He'll be alright. Just chill."

Tyrone reentered the room and tossed a ballooned plastic sandwich bag onto the coffee table. "Check it out. Prime stuff. And I packed it fat."

Brad opened the baggy and inhaled. "Ahh. That's nice."

Dylan said, "Looks good, T."

"Yeah, we like it, but four grand is kinda steep. Can't cut us a break?" Brad asked.

"This ain't a swap meet. Take it or leave it."

Brad bounced the bag in his palm. "Four thousand dollars. That's a lot of money. Not even sure we got that much."

"Well, that's a lot of Blitz. Don't pretend like you don't have it."

Dylan's smile gave it away. Brad told him, "Pay the man."

Tyrone sat in the chair opposite the couch and counted the bills Dylan handed over. "Well, it was nice visiting, but don't you guys think you should haul ass?"

"What's the rush?" Dylan asked. "It's barely nine. We're big boys. No curfew in college."

"I'm getting out of here. Should have already been gone. Got to get to my girl's."

Brad made a whipping motion. "Whi-pish, whi-pish."

"You guys are idiots. I ever tell you that?"

"Every week," Brad said. "How 'bout we smoke real quick before we jet? You know, try the goods."

"Don't think so, fellas. You got to go."

"Come on, brother," Dylan begged. "Just one bowl, we swear."

"Yeah, one bowl. Come on, dog."

"I'm running a business, not a crackhouse. Take that crap somewhere else."

"Alright, so let's talk business. Forty bucks so we can get lit real quick."

"You dude's are crazy. You want to smoke now?"

Brad pulled a small glass pipe from his front pocket. "Hell yeah. We got a deal?"

"Thought you guys didn't have any more cash."

"I just remembered we had a little left over."

"Forty each and you leave the second you're done. No bullshit."

"Cool. Give him the money, Dee."

"Why do I always gotta pay?"

"Because I don't have any cash on me. Just pay him. And give me your lighter."

Tyrone took the money and watched as they took turns ripping hits off the pipe. He waited until the bowl was burned to ask, "You guys really don't have any idea what day it is, do you?"

"Sure." Brad packed another bowl. "It's Tuesday."

"Nah, man, I think it's Wednesday," Dylan said. "Yeah, it's Wednesday, I bet."

Tyrone shook his head. "It's Tuesday."

Brad smacked Dylan's shoulder. "Told your stupid ass. Wednesday. What an idiot."

"I meant the date. What's today's date?"

Brad set the pipe down and pulled out his phone. "It's the first. August first."

"Doesn't that date mean anything to you?"

Both boys shook their heads.

"You guys never watch the news?"

Brad said, "That shit's too depressing."

"And boring. Can't stay awake watching that crap."

"Well, let me give you a clue. Today is the start of a certain season. Any ideas?"

Dylan bounced on the couch. "Oh shit, that's right. It's hunting season. I forgot all about it."

"Damn, you're right. Can't believe I forgot. My dad was just cleaning up his guns. He's got the fridge packed full of beer, too."

Dylan asked, "Why didn't you go with him?"

"Man, I want to like you can't believe, but I still got over a year before I hit 21. You're lucky, you only got a couple more months. Shit, you might be able to catch the end of this season. When's your birthday?"

"Day before Halloween. I ain't spending that kind of cash for two days of hunting. Plus, my dad isn't into that. Says he's against the hunt."

"Bullshit. He's just scared of getting shot."

"No way." Dylan thought about it and a smile crept across his face. "Yeah, you're probably right. It's not like he gives a rat's ass for them."

Brad stopped chuckling when he realized Tyrone was glaring at them. "What? What's wrong now? You're too uptight, man."

"I'm just dumbfounded that you admitted that in front of a black man with a gun. You must be high."

Dylan burst into laughter. "Dumbfounded. Dumbfounded. Who the hell says dumbfounded?"

"Big deal, Tyrone. The hunt's cool. It's always on the news. Helps the government, too. What's wrong with being patriotic?" Brad asked.

"Dumbfounded."

Brad elbowed his friend in the side. "Chill, dude."

"Patriotic? You want to help the government?" Tyrone said, "Why not donate money?"

"I'm not giving money away, and neither is my dad. It's our money and we'll spend it how we want."

"How'd your dad earn his money? The war, right?"

"I guess."

"And your dad?" he asked Dylan.

"Something with the trade embargoes. Practically made him a billionaire overnight."

"Hard-earned money. While the rest of the country is sunk in poverty, a handful of rich pricks like your daddies and the rest of your neighbors make it big. Capitalism at its best. And you guys think that's fair? Think that's cool?"

"I ain't complaining," Brad said.

Dylan laughed.

Tyrone pulled the gun out of his waistband and set it on the middle of the coffee table. Dylan stopped laughing.

"Tell you what would be fair." Tyrone said, "Whoever gets the gun and shoots the other two gets to live. How's that for fair? It's right between us. Both of you are just as close as I am."

Brad held up his hands. "Hey, man, relax. We were just joking around. No need to get so serious."

"Hunting season is as serious a subject there is."

"It's only three months long," Dylan said.

"Yeah and guess why they picked August through October. You high sons of bitches got any idea? No. Well, May through July are the months with the highest birth rates so they're killing two birds with one stone."

Neither of them said anything.

"Are you two retarded or do you just not care?"

"I'm high is what I am," Brad said, "and this is too confusing. Hunting season is what it is and us talking about it ain't gonna change nothing. Gotta deal with it, that's all."

Tyrone shook his head. "You guys do know this is a DHZ, right? Hunting season started 20 minutes ago."

Dylan turned to Brad. "Dude, we didn't just put ourselves in a hunting zone. Holy shit. You got to be kidding. Right, Tyrone?"

"Afraid not."

Brad said, "You're just trying to scare us. We're not in any danger."

"Think what you want but it's time for you guys to go."

"You serious? You're gonna throw us on the street?"

"Damn straight."

Dylan said, "Dude, we're high."

"I didn't make you smoke. You begged me."

"Shit, well, let us stay a couple minutes. Try to get our heads right." Brad fished out his wallet and pulled out a hundred dollar bill. "Come on. At least let us watch the news."

Tyrone ripped the bill out of Brad's hand and stuffed it in his pocket. "Funny how you just keep finding money you swore you didn't have. You can watch the news until nine thirty and then you're out."

It didn't take long to find a news station covering the hunt. The female reporter said, "And just one more reminder, hunting season will start in two and a half hours."

Dylan smacked the couch. "We still got time. Let's go."

Tyrone said, "Notice how it's still light where she is? This is the five o'clock replay."

Back in the news studio, the anchorman said, "And this season a record number of licenses have been sold. More than the last three years combined. The White House announced earlier today that at this rate the deficit will be erased in another five years."

"Wow, that's great news, John," the blonde anchorwoman said. "And for those of you hunters out there, here is a map of all the Southland's designated hunting zones. As you can see, Pasadena had the most exterminations last year with 3,967, Compton was second with 2,676, and El Monte close behind with 2,602."

Dylan clapped Brad on the back. "Check it out, Brad. 576. That's nothing. Long Beach is one of the lowest up there."

The studio had turned to another correspondent in the field. The reporter stood next to an older white man, clad in black, who was inspecting weapons and placing them in the back of his SUV.

"I'm sure most of you recognize this man. He is Ed Danbury, last year's winner. Not only did he beat out all the California hunters, Mr. Danbury outhunted the entire nation, earning himself a free unlimited license for this season and a sizeable cash prize of $5 million."

Mr. Danbury stopped what he was doing and interrupted the reporter. "I spent $11 million on all those licenses. I don't want to appear ungrateful but it seems like they should've at least given me my money back."

The reporter said, "Well, you won't be spending any money this year. Unlimited pass. No heading back to the government center after every 50. With your kind of numbers, that must have been quite a few trips."

"Eleven trips, 546 kills."

"Exterminations," the reporter corrected. Five hundred forty-six exterminations. That's something else. The majority of them were in Compton last year. What about this season? Heading back there?"

"Nope. That's exactly what they're expecting. El Monte, Compton, and Pasadena are going to be on lockdown. You won't find a soul on those streets and every door will be double-locked. I'm going to Long Beach." He returned to loading his vehicle. "Easier to contain."

"Not afraid of ruining your chances at the record by giving away your strategy?"

Danbury set the assault rifle on the pile. "I thrive on competition. I encourage everyone to come on down. You new guns need to be careful though. Probably be best to stay by the city limits and wait for people trying to sneak through. Do that and we can all have a great opening night."

Brad turned to his friend. "You still think we're safe on those streets. We're screwed. We can't leave here."

Tyrone turned off the TV and picked up the gun. "But you're going to. You guys don't have to go home, but you got to get the hell out of here."

"Just so you can get some ass? Let us stay here," Dylan said.

"You're dumber than I thought if you think I'd risk running these streets for a piece. Her place is well fortified. The basement's got a steel door no honky's getting through. And if they do get through, I'm taking a couple of them with me."

"Take us. We'll pay you," Brad said.

"I got enough of your money. Get up."

Dylan said, "You gotta. You gotta take us."

"I don't have to do a damn thing." He leveled the gun at them. "What you need to do is get up and get out. I've already wasted too much time with you."

Brad could barely stand. All the strength seemed to have left his legs. Dylan wasn't looking much better.

"Head to the door," Tyrone ordered, the gun still trained on them.

Brad said, 'How 'bout we stay here? We won't mess anything up."

"I don't want you to and it wouldn't do you any good anyway. Someone will bust through that door before morning."

Dylan stood in front of the door. "It's better than being out there."

Tyrone pushed the door open. "You're probably right, but I don't care. You guys have spent so much time acting black, it's about time you live it."

On the porch, Brad said, "That's messed up, man. I thought we were cool."

"Wrong." Tyrone slammed the door shut and threw the deadbolt.

The bang echoed down the street. Halfway down the stairs, a spotlight illuminated them. Brad shielded his eyes and rushed down the staircase. Dylan pounded on Tyrone's door. Brad yelled, "Get down here, Dee! Come on!"

The spotlight was coming from the intersection where men were talking and a truck started.

"Come on, Dylan! They're coming. Get in the goddamn car."

Dylan ran down the stairs, the truck headed toward them, less than half a block away.

The truck was still about 20 yards away when Dylan reached the car. He tried to open the driver's door but it was locked. Brad yelled for him to hurry.

Gunfire erupted and a bright stream of red exploded from Dylan's forehead. Bullets ricocheted off the car's roof.

Brad ran to the next car and ducked below its windows. When the truck headed past him, Brad scrambled back the way he had come and hauled ass. Someone spotted him and the truck took off in reverse. The crack of gunshots echoed in his ears, but he made it to the corner without being hit.

After two blocks, Brad's legs felt like rubber, his lungs were on fire. He didn't know where he was heading, and the truck was less than a block behind him. He was deep in the city and couldn't make it out running. There was also nowhere for him to hide with the truck's spotlight illuminating the street.

When Brad rounded the next corner, he couldn't believe his luck. Parked in the middle of his street was a silver Suburban with the unmistakable license plate, GOTPAID. His father was here.

The truck squealed around the corner. Brad waved his arms in the air as he sprinted toward his father's vehicle. "It's me! It's me!"

The driver's door opened and his father popped out with his rifle on his shoulder. The blast blinded Brad and knocked him flat on his back. His blood streamed toward the storm drain as his father laughed and told his partner, "Not a bad start. Keep this up and I'll get my 50 by next week."

Numbered Days

I can't tell if it is day or night in this windowless room. I have no clue what time it is, but I've got a feeling the doctor will be coming back soon.

There's nothing to look at but the thick gray foam that covers the ceiling and all four walls. I've already counted and cataloged every bump and ridge on the thin sheet of milky plastic that covers the overhead fluorescent. And there's the camera with the speaker below it. If I faced forward, I'd be looking right at it.

Usually I just close my eyes. That way I don't have to look at anything, especially the counter. I don't like to look at the counter.

I used to watch the IV drip-drip-drip its way into my arm. I'd look for bubbles, hope one might find a way through the safety device and float its way into my brain. Painless.

But watching the IV measured time. One bag was six hours, four bags a day. And it's not like I need any reminders when the day changes. The doctor always makes sure I know.

I also stopped monitoring the IV because I don't need to see the leather band restraining my forearm to the metal chair. I can't even budge them. I gave up after three days, about the same time I went completely hoarse and stopped yelling. My arms, my chest, my waist, my legs. All strapped down, beginning to atrophy from inactivity.

I'd been in one of these chairs before, although that one didn't have a hole cut in its bottom so I could relieve myself into a bucket. It was after my first DUI, or maybe my second, when I got belligerent. That one time was all it took. I learned my lesson. Never again did I spit on a cop.

But this guy isn't a cop. He's not even a real doctor. He's a fucking dentist.

I've only got three teeth left, along with 29 holes, half of which must be infected. Twenty-nine teeth dissolved in that jar of cloudy acid on the counter.

Nine of my fingers make up part of the jar's solution. Never again will they hold a brush, caress a breast, scratch an itch. They're gone for good. My right pointer finger is the last one I've got. All that's left of the other nine is the charred mess surrounding the burnt bone of my knuckles. Oh, God, how they hurt.

I refuse to cry. No matter what he does to me, I will not cry.

It's time. I hear him coming down the stairs. He has the same blank stare he's had the last nine times.

It hurts to talk, with my tongue so swollen, and he never answers me, but I have to try. "Doc. Doc. Will you talk to me?"

He's got his back to me, arranging his instruments on the counter.

"I'll give you anything you want. Please, just stop this. I swear, I'll never tell anyone."

He keeps fiddling with his damned toys.

"Doc! Stop this!"

He looks over his shoulder, stares at me as if I were scum. "You don't even know my name."

I didn't recognize him until the third day, but I leave that out when I say, "I know who you are."

"Oh?"

"Your wife died. It was an accident."

"You killed her! You should be in prison."

"It was a terrible mistake. I've learned."

"You were arrested twice in the last year, and you had another accident three weeks ago. You'll never learn."

"It will never happen again."

"I know it won't. Now open wide."

The metallic contraption in his hands is like something out of a hardcore bondage video. It only hurts to fight it.

"Good. Nice and tight."

I can't talk, the cold metal pressing against my volcanic gums. I know what he's going to do, but it doesn't help.

These aren't the tools he uses in his real office. They're rusty and dirty, and haven't been cleaned in the last ten days. They sit on the counter, the blood and bacteria growing before my eyes.

His favorite is the rusty Exacto he twirls around in each abscess, but the corroded pair of pliers always comes first.

The pain is intense, but even worse is the sound of my tooth slowly tearing from the gum, its roots stretching to the breaking point and finally snapping free.

Two more pulls and I'm toothless. He holds the jar in front of me and drops it in, another permanent piece of me dissolving in the acid. At first I didn't know why he was doing it. The teeth I tried writing off as some weird dentistry fixation, but now I know better. He's destroying my identifiable remains, making me disappear.

I wish I could kick him. Punch him. Bite him. Something. Anything. But I'm completely helpless. My mouth is a throbbing pit, my hands just as bad.

The phantom itching in my missing fingers is always the worst when he picks up his foot-long shears, another relic from the garage. The dull blades had been stained green and brown from chopping branches and hedges. Now they're covered in shades of red: bright red from yesterday, a lighter red from the day before, a brownish-red from the first week.

I never know if he's going to make it a clean break or if he's going to take his time, slowly snipping away at the flesh and playing with the bone. With this damn thing in my mouth I can't even beg for him to do it quickly. All I can do is hope.

The blades bite into the sides of my finger just above my knuckle. Blood drips onto the armrest and then onto the concrete floor.

Finally, the finger's detached and in the jar, flesh and bone dissolving. He grabs the butane torch and readies the flame. The first two seconds hurt like hell and then the shock sets in.

The smell of my flesh burning had me throwing up the first two days. Now I'm sort of used to it. It still makes me sick, but it bothers him, too. He holds his hand over his nose and mouth while the flame's on me.

No more teeth. No more fingers. My ten days are done. I still have my toes, tongue, ears. My manhood.

I don't know if this is good or not, but he's taking stuff out of the room. Every other time, he left the equipment lying there in front of me. Now he's putting it outside the door. Out goes the torch, the pliers, the shears. Even the jar and the IV stand.

He pops the piece out of my mouth and readies a shiny syringe.

The injection doesn't hurt, the cool fluid pushing into my vein. He places another syringe on the counter. This one has its cap on.

I ask, "What was that?"

He undoes my forearm straps, then releases the one around my shins. He grabs hold of the harness and gives it a hard jostle. "You can undo these yourself."

I hold up my hands, no fingers to flip him off. "How?"

"Do you even know why it's ten days?"

I can't stand it when he stares at me like this.

"Look at me. Why did I give you ten days?"

Talking isn't going to help.

"That's how long my wife was on life support before I told them to pull the plug."

"I'm sorry."

"I'm sure you're sorry I'm doing this to you, but that's it. You only care about yourself."

"That's not true."

"Well, we're about to see how much you do care for yourself. Very shortly you're going to notice that it is becoming harder and harder to breathe. I can already see you're struggling a bit to get air."

I am feeling a bit winded, my throat swollen, the airway seemingly smaller.

"My wife couldn't breathe without life support. Unlike her, you're getting a chance. See this syringe here? The stuff in there will counteract the injection I just gave you."

It's hard to talk, but I manage to get out, "Give it."

"Give it to yourself. You have a few minutes."

He turns his back on me and closes the door, the click of the deadbolt sliding into place.

There's no guarantee that he's telling the truth about the other syringe, but my throat's getting tighter, my time's running out. The chest harness has two push-button locks, one on each side of my hips. I can reach them but have nothing with which to push them. My thumbs are the most prominent knuckles and my best shot. He took my left thumb first, so it shouldn't be as raw and painful as the other.

Pieces of charred flesh crack off on the hard plastic. Tears flow from my eyes, blood from my knuckle. God, it hurts, but I can't get full breaths anymore. I have to get free.

The lock pops open, but the other side's worse, my right thumb having been cut off yesterday. I try my other knuckles but they're too small and just as painful. Now my entire hand is a bloody mess. I keep trying with my thumb as I'm forced to sip air.

The lock opens and my chest is free. The seat belt is easy to open using my elbow. I'm light-headed and almost sit back down. But I can't. I need that syringe.

I try to grab it off the counter with both hands, but it slips between my knuckles. Using the bridge of each hand, I get the cap off, bending the needle in the process. Hopefully it will still work.

I pick it up between the bridge of my left hand and the knuckles on my right. It slips but I manage to jab it through my shirt and into my belly.

My palm's on the plunger when the intercom goes on. "I forgot to mention you need to get that into your vein."

I pull it out and try to put it back on the counter but it falls to the floor. I follow it, dropping to my knees, unable to continue standing even if I wanted. My throat is sealed off, no air getting through. Thirty or forty seconds is the most I've got left. I claw at my throat, want to tear a hole in it, but have no fingers to dig with.

My mind's fuzzy but I have an idea and lie on my side, put my arm on the cold concrete, next to the syringe. I align the needle with my vein. All I have to do is push it in.

It's in. Just push the plunger. It's down all the way but I don't feel anything. I still can't breathe.

There's a crack down the side of the syringe. On the floor near my arm is a pool of clear fluid. I can't breathe. Can't move. Time's up.

Dead to Me

Leonard stared at the red left-turn arrow, wishing he could will it green. He was running late and, judging by the thick layer of snow accumulating on the Chevette's hood, he had spent about five minutes waiting to get through the light.

This was what he got for leaving his house on Christmas Day. New York City traffic was always bad, but on holidays it was unbearable. He had tried explaining that to his mother, but she argued he lived less than five miles away and could walk it in an hour. If he couldn't make such a short trip to spend the day with her, he wasn't fit to be called her son.

Christmas used to be his favorite time of the year, the entire day, just him and his mother, eating cookies and sipping cocoa. But things had changed. Although he still loved his mother, he was always on edge around her, praying she wouldn't make him mad. Ever since he turned 44 in August, his tolerance for his fellow man, which had truthfully never been that great in the first place, had rapidly deteriorated. The slightest things enraged him, and instead of letting things slide, he was quick to act.

Leonard looked out the passenger window to see if those lights were still green. The idiot in the lowered Honda next to him was creeping into the intersection, angling his front bumper into the left turn lane. Leonard glanced at the teenage driver to see if he was really intending to cut him off. The guy wouldn't look in his direction as he inched forward until both front tires were in the crosswalk.

Leonard checked his rearview mirror for cops. He sat up in his seat and looked across the intersection. There was a homeless man standing on the corner imploring generous souls for cash. The passing cars were finally coming to a halt. No cops anywhere. He didn't want to have to handle this himself, but he had no other choice.

The light turned green, and the Honda shot into the intersection, whipping into the space Leonard's Chevette would have been in if he had tried to race the guy. Instead of following the painted arc, the Honda sped toward the corner as if the light post was a giant magnet drawing it in. With a thundering boom, the car plowed into the light, its front end hugging the thick, immovable post.

Once he was certain there wouldn't be an explosion, Leonard ignored the yellow light and entered the intersection. The Honda's rear end obstructed all of the right lane and part of the second. With some skillful driving, Leonard managed to squeeze past the wreck without damaging his paint job.

The beggar was pinned between the pole and the car, his chest and head lying on top of the crumpled hood. How tragic that an innocent person had to be killed in such a needless accident, just because some idiot was trying to save time.

Now that imbecile's head was stuck to the shattered windshield, his smashed face embedded in the safety glass. Whether the punk was rushing to some Christmas party or hurrying to church, he should have been more considerate. Leonard had witnessed dozens of fatal accidents in the past month, four just this morning, and absolutely none of them were caused by a considerate driver. All of the drivers could have prevented their deaths if they hadn't been so careless and irresponsible.

The accident was completely forgotten by the time Leonard turned onto his mother's rundown street with its dilapidated houses, most the size of his one-bedroom apartment. He wished he could afford to move her into a nicer neighborhood, but that dream went out the window when he lost his job at the post office back in July.

Leonard drove several blocks past his mother's house before he found a parking spot. He walked back to her house, carrying her present with both hands, thinking about his new custodial engineer position and just how unfair it was. He arguably had the hardest job at the law office, yet he was lowest paid and received absolutely no respect. The people in charge had no idea how difficult and unpleasant his position was, much less how indispensable. No one there ever picked up after themselves and he was positive no one would show up for work if he neglected the filthy floors and allowed the trash to accumulate. Custodians should bring home more than what those sharks did, but he would have been more than happy to make what he had at the post office.

All the wishing in the world wouldn't get him a raise. Leonard cleared his mind and rang the doorbell. In the minute it took his 70-year-old mother to shuffle to the door, he imagined all the terrible, hurtful things she might say. If he fortified himself by mentally abusing himself before she could, it took some of the sting off her cold comments. He couldn't allow himself to get mad at her. Not on Christmas.

The door opened. There was her scowl, her round, wrinkled face, surrounded by her halo of wispy white curls. She swiveled her body just enough so he could squeeze by, shoving him into the house. "You're letting all the damn cold in. Hurry up."

"Good to see you, Mom."

She slammed the door behind them and waddled into the living room. Mumbling loud enough for him to hear, she said, "Four-thirty. No respect. Late on Christmas."

"Sorry, Mom, but traffic was real bad."

She plopped onto the squished side of the flowered couch, the plastic cover crinkling. "You've used that excuse for the last four weekends." She nodded toward the package he was still holding. "Put that on the table."

Leonard set her present on the coffee table. "There were a couple accidents. People died."

"You've used that, too. Funny how many people are supposedly dying when you're on the streets."

"I'm not lying."

"Oh, you would never lie to me."

Sarcasm was his mother's favorite friend, a sharp knife she loved to twist and turn. Leonard took a deep breath and counted to five, blew it out. "I lied once."

"You mean I caught you once. That's all it takes to destroy trust."

"It was one time. I was embarrassed."

"You should've been. You were warned about doing that sort of thing." She grimaced, shook her head, those curls bouncing. "Disgusting. It made me sick."

"I was twelve. Curious," he said absentmindedly. All his life, his mother and others always said that he made them sick. He had never taken it literally, but maybe he should have.

"You should've known better and shouldn't have lied. I don't want to talk about it anymore."

"Well, I'm not lying about the accidents."

"Of course you're not, but that doesn't change the fact that the food's cold now."

"You cooked?"

"Cookies. They were warm 30 minutes ago."

"I like them cold."

"Then get them. You know where the kitchen is."

The cookies were lined on a tray, thick blue and pink frosting, no question they were store-bought. Leonard took a bite out of a blue one, used his tongue to wipe the frosting from the roof of his mouth. He told himself his mother meant well, her coldness was a result of the cancer. She wasn't always this mean, and even if she had been, she had the right to be cruel every once in a while. She raised him on her own and he wasn't the best child in the world. Instead of causing her more heartache, he ought to thank her for all the sacrifices she had made for him over the years.

"I didn't tell you to bring the whole tray. I don't want any."

Leonard set the tray on the coffee table and eased onto the recliner, a cloud of dust puffing up around him, but it was still better than sitting on the stiff plastic covering the sofa.

"Put them back, I said."

"Maybe I'll eat them all."

"You're fat enough as it is."

"I'm just a little pudgy," Leonard said.

"Pudgy. Hah. You're fat. That's probably why you're not married."

"That's not why, Mom."

"Cause you're fat and you like to touch yourself …"

Leonard sighed. "One time. It was one time."

"Then why'd you lose your job for stealing those nudie magazines? Because you touch yourself," she said, shivering in disgust.

"I didn't steal anything, Mom." Leonard pinched the webbed area between his thumb and pointer finger, while in his mind chanting, *Om.* To his mother, he said, "Frank was a goddamn liar."

"You watch your mouth! On Christmas," she said with a huff.

"I'm sorry, but he had it in for me; he said all Italians were idiots." Seeing she didn't take the bait, he added, "And that Sicilians were the worst."

"How convenient."

"What?"

"Calling a dead man a liar. Someone who can't deny it."

It hadn't been stealing because Leonard only took home the Playboys and other adult magazines that had been deemed undeliverable. "Think what you want then. I know it wasn't stealing."

"Yeah, they just fired you over hearsay. Or maybe you quit, thought you'd be more fulfilled as a janitor."

Mailman to mop boy had not been an easy transition, and she knew it. All those mind-numbing hours pushing a broom, cleaning toilets, emptying waste cans, picturing Frank's stupid fucking face and muttering to himself, "You're dead to me. Dead to me. Dead to me."

He repeated this mantra all of July and to the third Saturday of August. It was ten minutes after six, the start of Leonard's shift, and a few hours after the firm's retirement party for the number two partner ended. Vomit in the sinks, diarrhea in the toilets, used condoms in the boardroom.

That'd been the moment everything changed, a new level of hatred as Leonard chucked the trash can across the lobby, forgetting it was full, beer bottles and wine glasses shattering on the tile. Never before had he hated someone with such intensity.

"You gonna just sit there?" his mother asked, interrupting his thoughts. "Don't tell me you're on drugs."

"No, Mom, just thinking." About Sunday's paper, how it listed Frank's time of death at 6:10 Saturday morning.

"Well, all that heavy breathing makes you sound like a stuffy bear. You having heart problems?"

"Nope." And neither did Frank; death was attributed to natural causes for one of the healthiest guys Leonard knew. The same went for his high school bullies, Tommy, Leroy, and Richard who were six feet under after Leonard focused on them for two weeks. "The breathing keeps me calm. Been practicing it in yoga."

She cackled. "You? Yoga?"

"I stream classes on my laptop."

"You wear leg warmers?"

Leonard didn't blame her for laughing. "Yeah, yeah, yeah. Doctor's orders, Mom."

"You said your heart was fine."

"It's just an expression. It's what I need to stay calm."

"And what good does that do you? Never heard of anyone doing anything worthwhile by staying calm."

Experiments on a couple of choice teachers convinced Leonard it wasn't a coincidence. By the end of September, his powers were so polished he took out each new subject within two days. Learning to harness the hatred had radically sped up the process. "I can be dangerous if I'm angry."

She rolled her eyes. "Did you start taking karate?"

During October he honed his methods and could eliminate someone in under an hour. In November he was down to ten minutes, but he was finding it more and more difficult to find people that had really pissed him off. He'd even brought out all his yearbooks to jar his memory about any wrongdoings. November saw the advent of the 30-second termination, something Leonard was incredibly proud of.

December was when the problem began. He had sharpened his mind into a perfect scythe, yet he lacked control. If Leonard didn't have his guard up, the slightest thing would set him off; and if he was set off, the offender was instantly dead.

"Why do you even come over if you're just going to sit there?"

Leonard shoved the anger down. "Come on, it's Christmas."

"So? What does it matter what day it is? You'll always be a disappointment." Her face turned a bright red. "Whether it's Sunday or Monday or Tuesday or Wednesday, or if it's Easter or Christmas or Veteran's Day, you'll always be you. I wish you had never…"

"Stop!" Leonard shouted a fraction of a second before his mother collapsed on the couch, the impact of her head a dull thud on the arm rest.

Leonard unclenched his fists and took five deep breaths, walked over and closed those anger-filled eyes. He picked a pink cookie off the tray and devoured it with a reminder he could not risk hating himself. He wasn't sure of the scope of his newly developed power, but it was still way too unpredictable to risk turning on himself.

Last in Line

Warren Zeller clenched his fists as he stood at the back of the line that wound its way through the dark alley. He'd been the last in line all his life. In elementary school, everything was done in alphabetical order. In junior high, before his growth spurt, he was picked last for every sport. In high school, he was the last guy to kiss a girl, and, last by far, to get laid.

When he grew older and realized that no one gave two shits about him, Warren took fate into own hands and joined the Cabrera Cartel, one of the most feared organizations on the East Coast. Sure, for the first couple of years, he was always last to benefit, but, as the sole white guy in a Columbian organization, that was to be expected.

In the beginning, they fed him table scraps and only allowed him glimpses of the beautiful whores the cartel shared like other families might share a remote control. He was the last to pick from the spoils of any robbery, and considered himself lucky whenever he got a taste of uncut cocaine. But Warren persevered and undertook every assignment with such enthusiasm and conviction that soon he was respected and even feared by the same men giving him the commands. No one tortured and killed like Warren, and those that did not know of Warren's reputation could take one look at his hardened face and realize they should stay the fuck out of his way.

But somehow, despite all the advances he'd made in his life, here he was once again, the last in line. Even though Warren couldn't remember why he was in this ridiculously long line, he wasn't about to tolerate it. He'd spent his whole life clawing his way to the top and he wasn't about to wait behind a bunch of pathetic losers.

Warren stepped to the side of the unmoving mass and peered down the dark alley, unable to see the head of the line. At first, he had thought they were waiting to get into an exclusive nightclub, but half of the people in line were degenerates in ratty clothing. In harsh contrast, many others wore business suits, and the remainder looked like average suckers you'd see walking the street.

This wasn't the first time that Warren had regained consciousness without being able to remember what he was doing or how he had gotten there. That was one of the drawbacks of using so much blow. He hated when this happened, but the journey was so much more enjoyable when his head was in a white cloud. When he was high, he didn't think about his repulsive face. He didn't think about his tiny cock. He didn't think about how the others in the cartel laughed at him behind his back because they were too afraid to do so in front of him. All he thought about was the next job and how good it would feel to end that person's life. Sometimes he'd even get hard when he considered new, exciting, and oh-so-painful ways to kill.

Fists still clenched, Warren shouldered past the scrawny man in front of him. He didn't look to the guy for an okay. He didn't say excuse me. He simply pushed ahead, knowing that the guy would either be a wimp and let it slide, or he would open his mouth and get a fist rammed down it.

Predictably, the pussy didn't say a word. Neither did the next five guys standing silently in line. As he moved forward,

Warren checked their faces, hoping to jar his memory. It wouldn't do for him to get inside wherever they were headed and not remember who he was there to kill.

Upset at himself for forgetting the identity of his target, Warren bumped the big, leather-clad biker in front of him. The six-foot-six giant turned around and glared at Warren. Not one to back down from a confrontation, Warren stared back and waited.

When the big man broke eye contact, Warren said, "Tell me where we're going and how long you've been in line."

A mocking smile crept across the biker's face. "You're standing in line and you don't know why?"

Without warning, Warren threw a vicious roundhouse, cracking the guy's jaw with a loud snap, and dropping him to the trash-strewn concrete. With the spectators too scared to stop him, Warren launched steel-toed kicks into the giant's face until it was unrecognizable. No one said a word as the wet thuds muffled the sound of breaking bones.

Warren stopped the attack and walked down the line just waiting for some other asshole to question him. It didn't take long before a punk in a cheap pinstripe stuck out his arm and said, "Where do you think you're going?"

The guy obviously hadn't been close enough to see the savage beating Warren had just handed out, but that was no excuse. When someone poked their nose where it didn't belong, they had to pay the price.

Warren hooked his arm over the guy's forearm and jerked backward, snapping his elbow, bending it in a direction God never intended. Before the guy could scream, Warren slammed his forehead into the guy's mouth, knocking out several teeth.

Not one to leave a job unfinished, Warren bashed the guy's head into the brick wall until it was the consistency of a rotten cantaloupe.

Warren wiped blood and brain matter onto his slacks and shouted down the line. "Who else thinks I should stay at the back of the line? Huh? Which one of you pussies doesn't want me cutting ahead?"

He glared at the line, daring someone to say something. Instead, everyone lowered their heads in submission.

Taking his time, Warren stalked down the dark alley, hoping someone would challenge him. He also hoped his mind would clear and he could remember why he was in the goddamn line in the first place.

As he neared the entrance where guards were slowly letting people through a red door, Warren finally remembered the identity of his target. Bobby Mendoza had intercepted two of the cartel's shipments, containing over two million in cash and coke.

Warren picked up his pace, strode up to the larger of the security guards, and demanded to be admitted.

The guard held up his hands and smiled. "I've got no problem with that." He pointed over Warren's shoulder and said, "But that guy might."

Anticipating a sucker-punch, Warren turned with his hands up. It was Bobby, patiently waiting at the front of the line. He recognized Warren but didn't seem concerned in the least. He also didn't reach for a weapon, almost as if he had already accepted his impending death.

Wanting a fair fight was never one of Warren's weaknesses. In his line of work, it didn't matter if your target was ready. It didn't matter how you won. This wasn't some duel out in the desert. You take your target out quick, before he knows what hit him. When the slightest error could end up leaving you dead, permanently injured, or in prison, you couldn't waste time on ethics.

Bobby was one hell of a knife fighter, and it would be smart to keep out of reach. This job required one well-placed bullet and a quick escape, leaving eyewitnesses confused and scared. Warren reached for his waistband, but his .40 wasn't in the holster. It didn't make any sense. Warren would never leave the house without his piece, and he couldn't remember dropping it.

His stomach clenched in anticipation of a plunging knife, but the strike never came. Bobby stood motionless and stared at Warren with vacant, resigned eyes.

Warren threw a crushing elbow across Bobby's face, sent him stumbling. A crowd formed behind Bobby who held his nose to stop the blood flow. Warren reached down for his ankle holster, but his backup wasn't there either.

Bobby held up his hands and said, "Hold up, man. There's no need to do this again. Go on in, Warren. You deserve to go ahead of me anyway."

Warren now noticed that Bobby's once-white dress shirt was stained crimson and riddled with over half a dozen bullet holes. A fuzzy memory of knocking Bobby to the ground and emptying his gun into him left Warren speechless. At first, he thought it was a dream. But Warren now clearly remembered standing over Bobby, firing round after round into him.

"I killed you," Warren said, confused.

"No shit."

"What are you doing back?"

"Who says I'm back? I'm just waiting my turn."

Warren glanced at the red door and the two guards standing on either side, beckoning Warren to enter. "For what?" He turned back to Bobby. "What's in there?"

"The place you've been hurrying to get to. All your life you've worked toward getting here, and now it's finally your turn. By all means, you should go ahead of me."

Warren replayed the memory. After shooting Bobby, he had sat down on the curb and dropped his backup .38 onto the street. It wasn't like him to stay around after a murder, especially such a noisy one, but he was lying down on the cold sidewalk. His chin dropped to his chest. There were several punctures in his torso, the hilt of Bobby's blade stuck deep between his ribs.

Warren shook his head to clear the memory. The knife was still lodged in his heart. He ripped it out and tossed it down the alley. One guard called his name while the other opened the door, a wave of heat smacking Warren in his face. The larger guard smiled and motioned Warren forward.

The Feeling's Back

Tiny flickers of energy tease the tips of my fingers, the tingling sensation the strongest it's been since I first noticed it three days ago. The feeling is back; there's no denying it.

This chair is painful to sit in, the hard oak digging into my back, but it's the only piece of furniture in the entire house I can get out of without assistance. I put aside my discomfort and concentrate on the ends of my fingers. It isn't my imagination. I'm regaining the use of my hands and arms. Life's about to change drastically, and I can't fucking wait.

The rickety TV tray is nestled beside the chair, ready to topple over if I rock too much. All that's on it is a journal I can never put my true feelings in and my Xanax bottle with the child-proof cap, complete overkill seeing how I can't pop the top off a can of Pringles.

I don't need a clock to tell me it's way past pill-time, and my stomach won't stop grumbling because all I've had is a tiny breakfast bar. Donna should've been back from the supermarket, but I'm betting she stopped by Hamburger Heaven to visit her new friend, Jennie. She'd been doing that a lot lately.

My anxiety's been through the roof the last few days, and having the bottle just sitting there only makes it worse. Plus, I need to take a piss. But if I'm going to be honest, those aren't the real reasons I'm upset she left me home like a newly house-broken dog. It's because I've been afraid I'd jinx myself if I told her the feeling is back. But that's just a stupid superstition. I'll tell her today as soon as she gets home.

My low back's begging for me to get up and stretch, my bladder demanding I go to the bathroom. I refuse and sit still, promise myself I'll only wait another five minutes. Having to piss makes me picture the terrycloth towel Donna attached to the rim of the tub. Not being able to wipe my own ass is bad enough, but having to straddle the tub and drag myself back and forth on that towel is beyond humiliating. Donna says she'd never tell a soul, but that doesn't really make it any better.

The crunch of Donna's Lexus pulling into the driveway helps me to feel more forgiving. Sure it sucks rubbing myself raw on a piece of glued down terrycloth, but cleaning my ass can't be one of her favorite duties. And I'd never tell her this, but if our roles were reversed, I know where I'd be when it came time for her mess.

The feeling is back and I'll be able to tell her soon. That's all that matters now. She won't have to be my arms anymore, won't have to wait on me night and day.

The Lexus turns off and Donna's wooden clogs clunk off the concrete. Her clomp, clomp, clomp up the stairs has me imagining a Clydesdale coming to my rescue. She obviously isn't everything I'd want in a wife, but like they say, beggars can't be choosers. And I know better than anyone else that men with two useless arms are never choosers.

The knob rattles because she'd locked the door, even though I always ask her to leave it unlocked in case I have to leave quickly because of a fire or some other emergency. It's safe out here, a neighborhood where no one locks their doors. No one except my Donna.

There's a loud bang on the door frame. "Terr Bear," she calls out sweet as rancid honey. "Terr Bear, open the door, will ya?"

That can't-believe-you-keep-calling-me-that feeling surges through me. It's not just the name, even though I absolutely hate it. She has the keys and two good arms to use them. But you can't tell that to a woman who just gave up her job and used half of her inheritance to buy a house for some cripple she'd only just met.

The negative thoughts won't help, so I bend forward at the waist and bite the rope dangling from the ceiling. Like a well-trained pitbull, I pull myself out of the chair and head for the kitchen. I brace against the door and raise my knee, poised to knock the deadbolt back.

Donna bangs on the door and shouts my name. The fingers on my right hand jerk into a fist but return to their useless state so fast I question whether I imagined it. My hand's just hanging but I can feel the faintest pulse in my fingertips. The feeling is back, stronger than ever, and not even Donna can ruin that. In my most pleasant voice, I say, "It'll only be a second."

It takes all my concentration to block out the metal digging into my kneecap, but I release the lock and take a step back.

Donna opens the door and greets me with a grin, half of a cheesy fry protruding from the corner of her mouth. In one hand is a shopping bag, in the other a grease-soaked brown paper bag whose saggy bottom is going to rip any second. She wobbles into the kitchen and sets down the groceries, the reek of her Estee Lauder triggering my headache.

She gulps the fry and gives me a peck on my cheek, smearing her bright-red lipstick so I'll have to beg her to wipe it off. She tosses the brown bag on the counter and says, "Stopped by to see Jennie and picked you up a burger."

"Thanks, but I'm trying to watch my weight," I say, staring at her calculating eyes, afraid any glance at her double chin, triple belly, or thunder thighs will make her think I'm judging.

The top of the bag's open, but Donna slices through the soggy bottom with her hot-pink fingernail. "Your loss." She pulls out the double-bacon cheeseburger and says, "I forgot you were trying to get back to your fighting weight. Got any bouts lined up?"

I keep my mouth shut, watch her stuff hers, a large glob of grease squeezing out the corner and dripping onto her too-tight shirt. I step back and keep the smile on my face, wondering if I can clench my fist and hold it long enough for her to see. For someone who'd spent most of her life as a caretaker, it seems she'd be more thoughtful. She hadn't been this hateful before we got married, so I'll write it off as resentment and do my best to keep my temper in check. "No, I don't plan on fighting again, but I've got to make sure I watch what I'm eating. Walking only burns so many calories and—"

"I know, I know," she mumbles around the burger. Donna pulls a two-liter Diet Coke from the fridge and drinks straight from the bottle. She smacks her lips and says, "I still got groceries in the car. Do me a favor and bring them in."

"Is the trunk open?"

Donna nods and pours the rest of the Coke into a large plastic cup.

I toe open the kitchen door and head outside, biting my tongue. I can't let her ruin my mood and I need to consider what would happen if I'm wrong about the feeling. What if it goes away?

In the backseat there's a crumpled brown bag, the bottom of it still wet with grease. I don't care if she wants to keep eating that crap, but I don't want to hear her bitching about not losing any weight. A little exercise, like getting these bags, wouldn't kill her either.

The trunk is barely cracked open. If I try pushing it open with my knee, I risk it snapping shut. But if I ask Donna to open it, I'll never hear the end of it.

My right hand hangs by my side like it's feeling something in my pocket. I concentrate as hard as I can and the tips of my fingers curl. My fist closes and opens. For the first time in over a year, my arm bends at the elbow. It's almost like I'm watching someone else as my hand goes under the trunk's lid and nudges it up.

The trunk only rises a few inches, but enough so I can get my knee under and raise it all the way. I'm tempted to see if I can haul a bag of groceries, but opening the trunk has left me drained. I bend at the waist and fish the handles of one of the bags into my mouth. There are five more, so I grab another. With the handles secured in my mouth, I lift them out of the trunk and head toward the kitchen.

The bags bounce off my chest and the handles dig deep into the corners of my mouth as I climb the stairs. I'm two steps from the kitchen counter when the bag hanging to my right rips. A carton of rocky road ice cream, two boxes of Hot Pockets, and a bag of frozen chicken wings smash on the floor.

I swing the intact bag onto the counter and say, "I'm sorry."

Donna turns around, the last bit of burger clamped between her fingers, the look of irritation I'd grown accustomed to.

Instead of pointing out that it wouldn't have happened if she'd done it herself, I say, "At least nothing broke."

Donna polishes off the burger, wiping her hands on her jeans. "I still gotta pick them up." She bends over with a sigh. "I'll get the rest of the bags."

"You sure?"

She sets the spilled food onto the counter. "Just go. Go watch TV and let me do everything."

Without a word, I turn and head out of the kitchen.

"I shouldn't have snapped at you," Donna says, her way of saying sorry. "I'll put the food away and bring you your lunch."

I head for the hallway and say, "It's no big deal," hiding the fact that I'm seething.

The bathroom door is closed even though she knows better. Tired of being a nuisance and relying on her for everything, I will both hands forward, surprised to see them moving so soon after the trunk.

My hands grab the sides of the knob and turn until the latch clicks free. I don't shout and brag about it, just enter the bathroom, wonder if I have the strength in my fingers to peel off that dingy strip of terrycloth attached to the rim of the tub. That little piece of shit-stained fabric sums up the last six months of my handicapped life, and I want more than anything to rip it free and tear it into a thousand bits. But that will have to wait.

Normally I'd have to lift my leg and catch the bottom of my basketball shorts on the hooked wire Donna installed for just that purpose. Instead, I concentrate on my dangling right hand, curl my index finger around the fabric and raise it so I can piss on my own.

Excited by my accomplishment, I drop my shorts before the pee trickles out. But even as the small circle of urine spreads on the front of my shorts, I can't help but smile. The feeling is back and there's no stopping it.

I close the door and head for my chair, ease into it barely aware I'm using my left hand to steady myself. I imagine the new recliner I'll buy; one of those cushy, leather jobs that'll wrap itself around me like a giant marshmallow.

Donna's still in the kitchen slapping together a sandwich of peanut butter and strawberry jelly on white bread, which she swears tastes 20 times better than wheat. I glance at my Xanax, thrilled I won't need them again after today.

She comes over with the paper plate and huge cup of Coke, and I put on my best smile. She sets it on the TV tray, pulls over the steel-reinforced chair so it's facing me, close enough so she can feed me, wipe up, and treat me like a helpless infant.

Instead of sitting in her chair, Donna plops on the armrest of mine. Before we tip over, she scoots back and puts her weight on me. Not aware, or maybe just not caring, that I can barely breathe, she smothers me with a hug and whispers that she loves me.

"Me too," I say, being sure not to breathe too deeply. This close, her perfume does little to mask her poor hygiene. Donna isn't very fond of bathing and the black rings filling the fat folds of her neck are making me nauseous.

Donna squeezes me again. "Did you see I made your favorite?" she says as her giant boobs press against my face and strands of her oily hair stick to my forehead.

Having to eat something all the time doesn't automatically make it your favorite, but I keep quiet, wishing I could bring my trapped arm up and push her away. Trying to sound sincere, I say, "Thanks. Would you mind getting me a drink to go with them?"

Donna squeezes me one last time before heaving herself to her feet. She lifts her cup off the tray and brings it to my lips. "Here you go. Take a sip."

I pull my head back. "That's not diet, is it?"

She takes her time before answering like she was thinking of lying. "A little won't hurt you."

"I hate to be a pain, Donna, but I hate that stuff."

Donna sighs and slams the cup onto the tray, drops of the sticky soda splashing out and landing on the Xanax and writing journal. "Are you serious? I've been running errands all day."

"Please," I say, wishing she wouldn't make me beg. "I have a hard time taking my pill with that stuff."

"I don't see how it's any different."

"Trust me on this one."

Donna's face hardens into a scowl. She's about to say something, but I beat her to it. "I've got some incredible news for us and—"

"What?" she asks with the excitement of a child. "What is it?"

"I want everything to be right before I tell you. Could you get that drink for me?"

Donna heads for the kitchen, her legs swishing together as she waddles away. "This had better be good."

"It's better than good." I flex my fingers and watch her as she searches for a clean cup. Just like I figured it would, it takes her more than a minute to get my drink, leaving me plenty of time to gather my thoughts and see just how much I can do with my hands.

Shortly she is standing there with my drink. "So what is it?"

I nod toward her chair and tell her to have a seat. "I'd like you to write it down for me."

Donna says, "No problem. Just tell me what it is."

"You'll see." I wait for her to pick up my journal and the pen clipped to it. "Our lives are about to change."

Donna puts pen to paper. "Did you win the lottery? What the hell is it?" she asks impatiently.

It feels good to finally be in the driver's seat, to have something she wants. "Let's just say it's good enough to deserve a toast. What do you say?"

Donna clinks our glasses together and puts mine to my lips for a sip before gulping down half of hers. "Here's to good news. God knows we can use it."

"Remember, word for word." I motion at the journal. "Start with a fresh page, please. This is special."

Donna nods and tells me to hurry.

"The feeling's back, and stronger than ever."

Donna looks up from the journal. "What feeling?"

Instead of answering her, I continue my speech. "I can't remember the last time I felt like this. But the pain is so intense."

Donna gasps and sets down the journal so she can pick up the bottle of pills. "I totally forgot." She struggles to get the cap free. "Here you go."

"It's fine. Just put the pills down, Donna. I'll have one when we're done with this."

"You sure?"

"Positive. Can I go on?"

Donna sets the bottle down, reads what she has on the paper and looks up. "The feeling. It's in your hands?"

I smile. "I can't wait to open this damn bottle. I'll do it soon. I'll take off the top, reach in, pull out one pill after another, stick them all on my tongue and wash them down with a drink of water from a glass I filled. A glass I held."

"I can get one for you real quick."

I ignore her and wait for her to take another drink before I say, "It feels so good to know I will never have to depend on anyone again." When Donna's pen stops moving, I ask if she got it all down. "You feeling okay? You're starting to sweat."

Donna wipes her slick forehead with the back of her arm. "I'm fine. Just got a little dizzy. Tell me that last part again."

I repeat the sentence, watching her pen shake ever so slightly as she writes down my words. She often pretends to be sick to get sympathy, but I know she's not faking now. "Can you finish? I'd really like to get this down," I say as gently as possible.

She looks up from the paper, her eyes filled with tears. "Are you telling me that you don't need me anymore? You don't want me? Is this your way of leaving me?"

"No, darling, it's not that at all. This is good news. I'll finally be able to do things for you."

A shiver courses through her, the fat folds rippling. She continues as if she hadn't heard my response. "I gave up everything for you. Everything. My job. My friends."

"You're upsetting yourself over nothing. Slow down and take a drink," I say.

Donna, who looks ready to lose her lunch, polishes off the rest of her Coke and sits there staring past me.

"Aren't you happy for me?" I ask, bringing her attention back.

Her pupils fight to stay focused on my face. "I am. Just worried," she says, her words starting to slur.

"Write this down word for word and then you'll be done."

Once Donna's ready, I say, "No one will ever have to worry about me again. I'll finally be free from this miserable life."

The pen is all over the paper, but even upside down I can read that the sprawling chicken scratch accurately reflects my words. "That's it. You can put the pen down."

The pen falls to the floor. Donna looks at the journal. "Can't read it."

"One last favor. The last one I ever ask. I swear."

She sets both arms on the TV tray to steady herself, her pupils completely dilated, jumping all around.

"Give me my pill. Then you can go to bed."

Donna reaches for the bottle and knocks it over with the back of her hand.

"Concentrate, Donna."

She uses one hand to steady the bottle and the other hand to pick it up, Donna unscrews the cap. She sticks her finger into the opening and pulls out half of a pill capsule, sets it on the tray. "This one broke."

"Try another."

With her eyes half closed, Donna blows out a breath and reaches into the bottle, pulls out three more empty capsule shells. "They screwed up," she says as she dumps the rest of the bottle onto the tray, broken shells spilling everywhere but no trace of the powder they once held.

I say, "We'll have to call the pharmacy and complain."

Donna sways back and forth in her chair, closing and then reopening her eyes. Struggling to get out each word, she says, "I got it yesterday. They were fine."

I scratch the side of my head. "You sure about that?"

"Your hand," she says before collapsing onto the floor.

The bottle rolls toward me and plunges off the edge of the TV tray. I nearly reach out and grab it, but it won't do to put my prints on the bottle I couldn't possibly have ever held.

I slip on the pair of latex gloves I'd taken from the bathroom and hidden in my shorts. Donna used to say that a guy with no arms could never have everything a man with both arms had. That might be true, but I have something others in my position would envy: an air-tight alibi.

There isn't a soul in town who isn't aware of my handicap. Not one person out there who doesn't shake their head when they see me and then laugh when I'm out of range. Everyone would swear what a nice guy I am, and no one would suspect I'd be capable of doing anyone harm.

I drop to a knee and pick up a pill shell that had fallen. Before I get up, I hold my hand under Donna's nose to confirm she's no longer breathing. If I were to call 911 right away, they'd probably be able to save her. I feel kind of guilty grinning about that.

I scoop up the rest of the pill capsules and place them in my pocket. I tear out each of the journal pages prior to Donna's suicide note, then head to the kitchen to start up the stove.

There's some great material in my hands, but I'd be stupid to keep them.

The journal pages and pill capsules are no more, the gloves flushed down the toilet. I take off out the front door for my daily walk, the time for me to greet my neighbors and let the world see what a miserable life I lead, unable to do anything for myself. None of them will suspect a thing. No one will be able to tell the feeling had come back. And no one will wonder why I decided to pick up and leave town soon after I found out my wife killed herself.

I keep the walk short, but it's long enough for the feeling to completely vanish, my arms and hands useless once again. I'm not discouraged though, and I'm not surprised. The feeling never stays long, but the nice thing is that it always comes back.

Dead Spot

Greg woke to a world of darkness and pain. He tried to open his eyes, but they were sealed shut with wet gunk. A sharp pain ripped through his shoulder when he tried to wipe them clear. His right arm was pinned beneath him, bent at an unnatural angle, but his left hand was free, able to clear the goo. Even with the blurry, double vision, Greg could tell it was blood. It was everywhere.

Afraid to move, Greg lay perfectly still. A steep incline of blood-splattered rocks rose less than a foot in front of him, a pile of broken branches inches from his face. A crippled sage bush lay on its side a few feet up from that. Something had run it over. Greg guessed it had been him.

The pain made it difficult to think. Something was wrong with his right leg, no feeling below the knee. His hip felt as if it were made of broken glass, and he was pretty sure something had punctured his stomach. A gentle feel found a branch over an inch in diameter sticking out of his side. Everything else seemed okay except for his face. It was resting on a rock, tender and swollen, a clear sign his jaw had been broken.

Whether it was the shock, the blow to the head, or the intense pain, Greg could not remember what had happened. He searched for a sign, something to trigger his memory. Rock. Dirt. Branches. Blood. He was a teacher. Math. Young kids, not quite sure of their grade. Fourth maybe. Definitely nothing to do with this place.

185

The sun hung directly overhead. It was work hours but he wasn't at school, so that meant it was the weekend. And he was at the bottom of a hill. There weren't any hills by his house. The closest place above sea level was Fallen Rock, an hour's drive from the city, far enough away that visitors were few and far between.

The distant sound of crying from above brought everything back. It was Heather, Greg's girlfriend of five years. They'd gone hiking. She'd been walking right behind him. Oh God. He hoped she hadn't fallen with him, that the entire path hadn't collapsed beneath their weight.

Greg lifted his head off the rock, then set it back down, nauseous from the movement. He tried to scream, but his lips wouldn't open more than an inch. His jaw had been shattered, not merely broken, and yelling was out of the question.

A soft sob drifted down the hill. "Oh God," Heather moaned. "Why?"

Greg reached for his cell phone, but his left pocket was empty and the right one was pressed against the ground. Greg lifted his hips off the ground. Crushed bones tore into his muscles and ligaments when he reached into his pocket and pulled out the phone.

The phone's display was cracked, but the power was still on. A dispatcher wouldn't be able to comprehend his mumblings, so Greg punched in 911 and began a text, struggling to type with his blood-slick hand.

Four words in, Heather screamed, "Die! Die!"

Greg tilted his head and followed the incline, the bloodied path he'd fallen. Heather stood at the top, some 30 yards away, hysterical, her hair wild as if she'd been pulling it out.

He raised the phone so she could see he was okay, that he'd get help for them.

"No!" She stomped her feet on the path. "Die!"

Greg's vision had cleared enough for him to understand he hadn't misheard her. He could see she was furious, not fearful.

Heather withdrew from the edge of the cliff, leaving him alone with his confused thoughts. Was it possible that he was so bad off that she was begging God for mercy, wanting Greg to die so his suffering would end?

Not ready to give up no matter how badly he was injured, Greg turned back to his text. Typing with only his left hand was taking too long. He'd only gotten out, "Need help – Fa," when he heard Heather return. She was back at the top of the cliff, holding the bottom of her shirt out in front of her, something heavy pulling the fabric down.

Greg wanted to tell her that he would be okay, for her not to worry, that he was sending for help. He'd make a full recovery and find a way to provide for her. He wanted to tell her how much he loved her, how she was the perfect woman for him, and he couldn't imagine living without her. Then she pulled something from her makeshift basket, cocked her arm back and threw it at him.

It crashed into the hillside right above his head. She had thrown a fist-sized rock at him. And she already had another one in her hand.

Heather let out a maniacal scream and threw the rock. It smashed into Greg's right shoulder, feeling like a baseball bat swung full speed. "Asshole. You think I didn't know what you were doing?"

187

Greg was terrified, no idea what she was yelling about. He loved Heather more than anything. He'd never done anything to hurt her.

The next rock whizzed by Greg's ear. The second grazed his thigh. She was throwing big rocks, and if one hit his head, he'd never survive.

"You think I'm stupid?" She threw a rock that ricocheted off the ground and struck Greg's swollen cheek, washing him in a crimson flood of pain. "I hate you! Die!"

It finally dawned on Greg that he hadn't tripped. The ground hadn't given beneath his weight. The crazy bitch at the top of the hill, the woman he had loved for the last five years, had pushed him.

The next rock struck Greg in the chest. Knowing he was dead if he didn't send the text, he resumed typing, holding the phone between his face and Heather, hoping it would deflect a head shot.

Heather ran away from the edge. Greg pressed the buttons as quickly as possible, not bothering to delete any errors. He'd almost finished when Heather returned with a loud grunt.

She was hunched over, her shoulders rising with each heavy breath, a large boulder between her legs. Greg shook his head, no longer feeling the pain. She shook her head back at him.

"Did you really think I wouldn't recognize my own sister's number? I saw the bill. I saw how many times you called her, how many times she called you." She gave a disgusted laugh. "How long have you been screwing her?"

Greg screamed an unintelligible no. He'd been talking to Beverly, Heather's younger sister, for the past few weeks, keeping it secret. She'd helped him pick out the ring and organize the surprise engagement party that they'd been headed to, where all their friends and family waited.

Heather placed her hands under the boulder. "I've been cheated on before. Too many times." She tipped the boulder over the edge. "But never with my sister."

The boulder picked up speed, bouncing right toward Greg. Before he could hit the send button, the boulder blasted into his forearm, snapping it in half and sending the phone flying.

Heather left Greg alone. He managed to move his numb hand toward the phone and hit the send button. The message came back that the text was not sent. There was no service.

Heather grunted from above. Maybe she'd stop if she saw the ring, knew he was serious, let him explain. But the ring had been in his left pocket which was now empty. The box had to have fallen out when he tumbled down the hill.

He spotted the tiny white jewelry box caught in the branches of the downed sage bush, too far to reach.

Heather appeared, out of breath, a giant boulder the size of her torso balanced on the cliff's edge. Greg grit his teeth, swallowed the pain and tried to point his shattered arm toward the ring. She didn't even look, her eyes fixed on his. "I hope she was worth it," she said between breaths. "This was."

All Greg could do was watch as Heather put her foot on the boulder and pushed it off the edge. It rolled, rolled, rolled, gaining momentum, bringing down the hillside with each big bounce, each thud vibrating through Greg's body. He tried to roll away, but there was no escape.

Left Unfinished

A soft scraping sound pulled Robert from his nightmare a little after three a.m. If he was lucky, he would catch a few more hours of sleep before the long day ahead. The novel had to be in Marty's hands by eight that night, and Robert wanted to proofread it one last time.

Robert closed his eyes and pulled the comforter to his chin. The metallic scraping returned, louder and longer this time. It sounded as if it were coming from inside the house. From inside his room.

The silhouette of a man appeared at the foot of his bed. A very large man. And the man was drawing something across the metal crossbar, just inches from his feet.

This was still a nightmare. Everything seemed so real, but Robert must have fallen back to sleep without realizing it. Either that or he never woke the first time. It was just a realistic dream.

Robert's eyes adjusted to the darkness and he realized it was the same guy from his nightmare, and he was dragging a straight-edge razor against the bed frame. No one used those kinds of razors anymore. Further evidence that this had to be a dream.

The scraping stopped and the man grasped the bottom of the comforter and tossed it onto the floor. The breeze from the open window blew across Robert's feet. If this were one of his novels, the hero would whip out a gun, but Robert was too petrified to even move.

The man grabbed Robert's foot and held it against his side, brought the razor beside it.

Robert clapped his hands and the bedroom lights flashed on. This couldn't be. The man didn't have a face, at least not a real one. Besides the black goatee and flattened nose, the rest of the bald man's features were not fully formed. The man's ears were large lumps with no real shape. His eyes were round and black, but dull and void of life. Instead of lips between the mustache and chin, there was only skin.

"Wake, damn it! Robert screamed. "Wake!"

The man squeezed his ankle harder, set the razor against the top of Robert's foot.

Robert tried to yank his foot back, but the mouthless man had it in a vice grip.

The razor bit into the top of his foot, slicing through the skin and veins, riding across the bone. The pain was so clear and brilliant. Robert rifled his free foot on the man's hand, knocking it away but not freeing the razor.

The bald giant held up a fist: a mass of flesh fused around the razor's handle. No thumb, no fingers, no knuckles. It was the right size and color of a fist, but it lacked all detail, unlike the shiny razor, which was identical to the weapon wielded by the villain from Robert's novel.

Robert continued to fight, but even with the blood lubricating his ankle, he couldn't pull free. Red hot pain ripped through his foot as the bastard tore open another gash. The creature's face couldn't show emotion, but Robert knew the son of a bitch loved every second.

The man finally let Robert's leg fall. Robert had never experienced such pain, part of him wanting to die, to surrender, but then he noticed the attacker's left hand. It had only one finger, the ring finger. And it had an intricately designed titanium wedding ring wrapped around it. He had a very bad feeling he knew what was inscribed inside it.

Looking the killer in his blank eyes, Robert said, "Larry, with this ring, I give you my soul. Forever yours, Veronica."

The man nodded and if he'd had lips, Robert was sure they would've spread in a grin.

Jesus Christ. It couldn't be Larry. Larry didn't exist. But neither did people who were missing mouths.

The man pulled the black turtleneck over his shaved head. The Southside Slasher always killed with his shirt off. He loved the feel of warm blood spraying onto his skin. And there they were. His tattoos. The snake wrapped around his left arm and the demonic skull on his right. Robert had drawn those tattoos himself and here they were, in the flesh.

The sleeve of the turtleneck got caught on the fist with the razor in it. Robert slid off the bed, nearly passing out from the pain when his injured foot hit the floor. Hopping on his good foot, Robert reached the bathroom as a muffled scream came from behind. He glanced over his shoulder and saw Larry tear the turtleneck in half as he howled, the skin covering his mouth muting the sound.

Robert slammed the door closed behind him and threw the lock a second before Larry crashed into it. Robert slid down against the door and grabbed the towels lying on the floor. He had already lost a lot of blood and couldn't last much longer if he kept gushing. With the handle rattling back and forth above his head, Robert made a quick tourniquet with one towel and wrapped two others around his wounds. He needed to get to a hospital.

The handle stopped turning and heavy footsteps left the room. There was only one door in the bathroom and Robert couldn't fit through the sliver of a window even if he had been a hundred pounds lighter. He was stuck in here and his cell phone was beside the bed. The closest neighbor was over a block away. He was screwed.

With his ear to the door, Robert could hear noise coming from one of the rooms. He had hoped against hope that Larry was leaving, but he knew better than that. He knew Larry better than anyone did. This guy was the definition of evil.

When Robert had created the serial killer, he had worried the character wouldn't be believable. Sure there were psychos and sociopaths that did some really outrageous shit, but Larry lived to take lives. He loved inflicting pain. Robert had been afraid he had made the guy too sadistic, too over the top, but his agent convinced him it would sell. Larry would make a figurative killing.

There was a loud grunt and the thump of footsteps heading toward the bedroom. He must've found something to open the door. What could Robert do? He had no weapons in here. He couldn't get away. He was helpless.

Why was Larry was after him in the first place? Robert had created the maniac. He had given him life. Larry survived at the end of the novel. There was the possibility of a sequel. Why would he come after his creator? And why was he deformed?

The footsteps stopped outside the door. Robert held his breath and waited. A thundering kick slammed into the door, knocking Robert toward the toilet. The door bounced off the bathroom wall and back into the frame.

The door thrust open. Larry stepped into the bathroom and set Robert's laptop at his feet. On his way out of the bathroom, Larry ripped the bathroom door off its hinges and threw it onto the bed. He grabbed the chair at the desk and plopped down on it outside the bathroom.

The only reason Larry wouldn't kill someone would be because he wanted something. He wanted something from Robert and it had something to do with the book.

Robert turned on the computer and opened the document, trying to block out the mind-numbing pain and concentrate on the story. What was there not to be happy with? Larry didn't die. He satisfied every vile urge he felt, four times alone in one chapter. The ladies found him attractive and charming.

Attractive. This guy wasn't attractive. Robert looked up and studied Larry. He could be attractive, if he weren't missing parts, if he weren't deformed.

That was it. It wasn't that Larry was deformed. He wasn't described. Robert had thought he had described him to a T, but looking back, he realized he may have rushed over some difficult spots and cut a few corners. Description had never been his strong point, unless of course he was describing a maggot-infested wound or the slow-motion bludgeoning of an old woman. Flowery descriptions were for the literary novelists. They could spend pages describing someone's eyes. He would mention the blonde's eyes were blue and rush to the good part where she was being ravaged by the madman.

"You want to be whole?"

Larry grunted with a nod.

Robert searched for the first mention of the maniac. "I guess step one should be give you a mouth." There was a weak paragraph where Robert added a short sentence describing Larry's razor thin lips that complemented his sharp tongue.

"Goddamn it, Bobby. It's about fucking time," he said in a girlish whisper.

Robert stared at the hulking beast.

"Fix it!" Larry shrieked.

Robert rushed to Larry's first kill and began typing. He'd always pictured the man with a rough, gravelly voice.

"Let's see," Larry growled. "Much better. Much better, Bobby-boy."

"It's Robert."

Larry pointed the bloody razor at him. "It's whatever the fuck I decide it is, Bobby-boy."

"Sorry."

"Should be. You know this is the first goddamn time I've talked?"

"No way," he said, still in disbelief he could be having this conversation. "You're the main character."

"And I talk to myself the whole time. Find me a place where I'm in quotes." Larry teased his nipple with the tip of the razor. "What's that, smart guy? Can't find one? Didn't think so. Now how about some goddamn fingers?"

Robert found the perfect spot to add the details. When he looked up from the computer, Larry flexed his fingers around the razor, the muscles rippling through his forearm.

"And my name. What the fuck is up with that? Lawrence. Larry. That's some gay shit. I need something tougher than that."

Robert sighed. "I gave you a good name. You're a regular guy. Your co-workers, your wife, your friends. They don't know you're a sadistic prick. You need a regular guy's name."

Larry tossed the razor into the air and caught it in his other hand. "I've never taken a life with my left. Don't make yours be the first."

"What name do you want?"

"You're the writer."

Robert didn't need to look up to know Larry was smirking. The asshole loved this. He didn't care that Robert hurt so much he could barely think. "How about Jack or Derrick?"

"How 'bout no. Damian. That's cool. Something like that."

Robert shrugged and did a quick Find and Replace. "Real original," he mumbled as he changed the name more than 300 times with the push of one button.

"Now hurry up and fix the rest of me. Some decent ears would be nice."

Robert always hated critics and Larry … Damian was getting on his last nerve. He tried not to smile as he described the necrotic ears barely attached to the man's skull.

"Hey, dickhead."

Robert ignored him and continued to type, giving Damian slanted eyes.

"There's a fucking mirror right behind you. Fix this shit or I'm going to fuck you up real bad. What I did to Mary will seem like a Sunday school lesson compared to what I do to you. And you know I can make you last as long as I want."

A shiver ripped through Robert's body. He had created a master of disaster, a doctor of pain. Damian thrived on torture, keeping his victims alive and conscious for every single ounce of fun.

Robert deleted his last sentence and watched Damian's eyes and ears return to their former state. He thought back to Mary's scene where Damian's actions had made her think he would let her live if she satisfied him. That possibility never entered Damian's mind. He never let anyone live. He gave them false hope to make their anguish just that much more beautiful. He wasn't going to let Robert live. As soon as he was finished so was Robert.

"Good job, Bobby-boy. Now I'll be a real lady-killer."

Robert set the laptop on the counter and pushed himself onto the toilet.

"Gotta shit? I think you can hold it."

"I'm trying to get comfortable." Robert put the computer back onto his lap. He had a plan and he hoped to hell it would work. If it did, he'd escape with his life and his story.

"Just hurry up. I got places to go and people to kill."

"I'm sure you do," Robert said as he positioned the cursor. He erased the hand description and heard the razor clatter to the floor.

"What the hell?" Damian growled, unable to pick up the weapon with either hand.

As calm as possible, Robert said, "Wait a second. I'm trying to fix you up. I got to turn this in tomorrow and we need you in tip-top shape."

"Hurry up," he said with a hint of nervousness in his voice.

"Not a problem." Robert added a word to Damian's description.

Damian yelled, "Put the lights back on! What the fuck! What the fuck'd you do?"

Robert exploded off the toilet and squeezed out the doorway, putting as little weight as possible on his ruined foot. He felt Damian reach for him, but the maniac's one finger wasn't strong enough to grab hold.

"You asshole! I'm blind!" he screamed as he shot out of the chair and lumbered after Robert.

Robert was opening the bedroom door when Damian got hold of him and slammed him into the wall. Robert fell to the floor and wrapped his arms around Damian's legs, trying to knock the man down. Damian, who hadn't lost his skills as a collegiate wrestler, sprawled and crushed Robert beneath him.

Keeping his weight pressed firmly against Robert's back, Damian said, "Fix it. Fix it now or I swear to God, I'll club you to death. Don't think I can't. I could choke you right now if I wanted to," he said as he slipped an arm around Robert's neck. "Give me back my fucking eyes."

"The laptop's under me."

Damian used his free hand to feel for the computer. He slid to Robert's side, keeping his arm around the man's throat. "Do it."

Robert had one shot left but it meant destroying an entire year's work. He'd be throwing away more than just a huge paycheck and a lifetime worth of royalties. He'd be destroying his baby, a piece of himself. But it had to be. It was the only way.

Damian tightened his grip. "What the hell's taking so long?"

"I'm finding my spot." White spots danced in front of Robert's eyes. He right-clicked the file and hit delete. "By the way, Damian. What were you going to carve on my stomach?"

he gasped while the computer asked if he was really sure he wanted to delete the file.

"Fix me and maybe I won't."

Robert knew that the man would. The madman carved epithets on every victim. He thought human flesh made a wonderful canvas, no better medium than a body. But it wouldn't be Robert's body. Not today.

Robert hit okay and Larry's arm pulled away from his neck. Robert took a breath and sat up. Larry was standing, looking down at him. His mouth was missing and the razor had magically found its way into the lump of his right hand. The file was still sitting in the recycle bin. Robert lifted the laptop into the air and brought it crashing down onto the floor. The computer was in pieces. The file was gone, Larry destroyed.

But he wasn't. Larry didn't have a mouth, and his eyes didn't show any emotion, but Robert knew the bastard was smiling. In the lump of his right hand was the razor. In his other hand, pinched between his one finger and palm was Robert's yellow backup flash drive.

Last Will and Testament

Death. It's what I write about it. It's what I've been thinking about since I can remember. It's what I wished for the first half of my life.

Now that I'm 47, death has become even more real, more of a shadow hanging over my head. I stay relatively healthy and grateful for what I have, always reminding myself I'm lucky to be alive and that nothing's promised. Except death. That motherfucker is guaranteed.

Even though I understand death's inevitable, I've never made a will. My wife often points out we should do one, and I always agree, but that's as far as we get.

But that's going to change because I've changed my perspective. Death doesn't have to be so depressing. It's just part of our cycle. We come into this world tearing skin, bathed in blood, and welcomed with screams. Why not go out just as gloriously?

Over the last year I've seen some cool stories about people making the most out of death. I applaud them. This is the one time in your life where you are truly the center of attention. Soak that shit up.

So for my last will and testament:

First off, I want to get the party started ASAP to keep me looking as fresh as possible. Ideally, I'd like to do the screening a day or two after my demise. Let's book a decent venue, something with a stage. Just please no Chuck E. Cheese.

The stage is important because that's where I'll be, everyone else down below. Instead of a casket I'd like to be propped up in a chair. I'm not too picky about what pose I'm in, but make it look natural, hands where we can see them.

We'll need a friend who will usher people up one by one to say goodbye. If people are feeling generous and would like to help pay for the funeral arrangements, they can stuff bills and personal checks in my pockets or down my shirt. If they're cheap or claim to only have credit cards, be sure to set up payments through PayPal.

It'd also be a good idea to hire a photographer to capture these moments; package deals and a la carte purchase options should be made available. I suggest giving each person up to three poses with me, and they can do whatever they want with my arms and legs. We can also use the best photos for a GiveMeYourMoney app to defray costs.

Some people in the crowd might not be cool with all this, so let's loosen them up with a little music, starting slow with some classical but transitioning smoothly to something peppy. That's when the DJ can play my prerecorded message, asking people to head to the dance floor. This is a time to celebrate, not be pouty and sad.

As soon as everyone's on their feet, it's time for the marionette show. I don't expect any fancy dance moves, but I want them making me look alive up there; at least *Weekend at Bernie's* quality.

The DJ will invite people to dance with me and offer one last goodbye, but a minimum payment will be required. After all, this funeral ain't cheap.

That will wrap up the screening, with everyone in high spirits. At this point it'd be a huge letdown to simply throw me in a fire or toss me in a hole and let maggots munch through my brain. Get me over to the tanner's so they can slice off my tattooed back piece and start the curation process, turning it into a cape that will be FedEx'd to the highest bidder about a week after the funeral.

Depending on the cost and time involved, we might as well slice off my other tattoos and see if we can't get something out of them, maybe a nice headband or two, or sew them together for a belt.

From there I'd like to be stuffed, maybe have the hole in my back patched up with a slab of fresh skin off someone else. I'm not sure where we'll be technology-wise when I blink out of existence, but I'm guessing we should be able to keep me in relatively good shape for at least a couple days. Last thing I'd want to do is start leaking all over the couch or recliner.

Ideally my family would be able to move me, reposition me, dress me as they see fit. Once I start to spoil or the family grows tired of me we prepare for one last hurrah.

Drones. Yep, they're not just used for killing people in foreign countries. I've seen videos of a guy flying his dead cat. A deer. A cow. So why not me?

If the whole stuffing process dries me out too much or makes a Mark drone impossible, then I'm fine scrapping the taxidermy because turning me into a drone has top priority.

Once they've scraped out my innards and replaced them with electronics, fuel, and explosives, everyone will meet us at the beach. It will be about an hour before sunset, time to start the campfire and tell stories over drinks.

When the sun begins its descent, my friends and family get a chance to fly me, one to two minutes each depending on available sunlight.

Once everyone has had a turn, my son can don my tattoo cape (and headband or belt) and take the helm. All the others will grab bows and arrows. If Jake throws a fit about it not being fair, someone please trade with him and let him take some shots. It might even be nice to let him have the first one.

For my final flight let's blast Iron Maiden's "Flight of Icarus," the entire event filmed from above and below in order to share on YouTube. Near the end of the song, everyone lights their arrows and I make my final climb toward the sun. Be sure to bring a lot of arrows in case people are drunk and terrible shots. The song will also loop in case this part drags. Eventually an arrow will hit, I will burst into flames, and a giant explosion will scatter my pieces over the sea.

This is my last will and testament, although I give my family permission to do whatever they see fit. My only rule is that no one take it too seriously. My run will be exactly as long as it needs to be, and I want everyone to know that I'm grateful for every minute of it.

REVIEW

If you enjoyed these stories, I hope you'll take a moment to write a quick review. As an independent author, word of mouth and reviews are incredibly helpful. Whether you leave one star or five, honest feedback is truly appreciated.

And if you're on Goodreads or BookBub please stalk me. I believe the technical term is Follow, but I strive on anxiety and what better way to amp it up than thinking there are hundreds of strangers stalking me. Plus, you'll be alerted to all my new books and deals. Sounds like a win-win to me.

Goodreads https://www.goodreads.com/author/show/6115084.Mark_Tullius

BookBub https://www.bookbub.com/authors/mark-tullius

OUT NOW

Ain't No Messiah

The coming of age story of Joshua Campbell, a man of death-defying miracles, whose father proclaimed him the Second Coming of Christ.

This psychological thriller takes us through Joshua's childhood of physical and emotional abuse at the hands of his earthly father, and into adulthood as Joshua attempts to break away from his family and church in order to find happiness.

Twisted Reunion

"Time-honored frights with innovation infused throughout."- *Kirkus Reviews*

Plunge deep into darkness with 28 terrifying tales. Explore heartache, happiness, and horror in this collection of all the stories in *Each Dawn I Die*, *Every One's Lethal*, and *Repackaged Presents*, plus two bonus stories.

25 Perfect Days: Plus 5 More

A totalitarian state doesn't just happen overnight. It's a slow, dangerous slide. *25 Perfect Days Plus 5 More* chronicles the path into a hellish future of food shortages, contaminated water, sweeping incarceration, an ultra-radical religion, and the extreme measures taken to reduce the population. Through 30 interlinked stories, each written from a different character's point of view, *25 Perfect Days* captures the sacrifice, courage, and love needed to survive and eventually overcome this dystopian nightmare.

Untold Mayhem

24 unique stories of madman and monsters. Crime stories filled with suspense, horror, and mystery. Immerse yourself into the world of untold mayhem.

Brightside

Across the nation, telepaths are rounded up and sent to the beautiful mountain town of Brightside. They're told it's just like everywhere else, probably even nicer. As long as they follow the rules and don't ever think about leaving. Joe Nolan is one of the accused, a man who spent his life hearing things people left unsaid. And now he's paying for it on his hundredth day in Brightside, fighting to keep hold of his secret in a town where no thought is safe.

Try Not to Die: In Brightside

Mark and 10th Planet Jiu Jitsu teammate Dawna Gonzales continue the Brightside saga, bridging the gap between the first book and sequel, this time from the eyes of a female teenage telepath.

Beyond Brightside

The exciting conclusion to the Brightside saga. Joe and Becky thought life was hard in Brightside, but beyond Brightside is even more brutal.

Try Not to Die: At Grandma's House

It's Grandma's House – quiet, cozy, nestled on a little mountain in West Virginia. What could possibly go wrong? A lot, actually.

So watch your back. Choose wisely. One misstep will get you and your little sister killed.

To survive, you'll battle creatures, beasts, and even your grandparents as you unravel the mystery of your older brother's death in this interactive, graphic novel.

Try Not to Die: In the Pandemic

Mark and John Palisano take readers on the most intense hour they will ever spend on a cruise ship in this non-stop interactive adventure.

Unlocking the Cage

For his first nonfiction project, Tullius spent 3 years traveling to 23 states and visiting 100 gyms where he interviewed 340 fighters in his search to understand who MMA fighters are and why they fight.

"The result is a surprisingly revealing read recommended not just for enthusiasts of boxing, fighting, and MMA in particular, but especially for outsiders who abhor the idea of such a sport without really understanding its players. This audience will find their eyes opened about many things, including evolving values and maturity processes in life, and will discover *Unlocking the Cage* also unlocks preconceived notions about a little-understood sport." - *D.Donovan, Senior Reviewer, Midwest Book Review*

COMING SOON

TBI or CTE: What the Hell is Wrong with Me?

An author with a reckless past set his fiction aside to tackle a critical mission: Help those around him struggling with head trauma and chart a way forward. But a fateful visit to the doctor upended his entire world...

Former fighter and Ivy League football player Mark Tullius wanted to support his friends with traumatic brain injuries (TBI) and chronic traumatic encephalopathy (CTE). But when presented with a scan of his own grey matter, his life changed forever. After years of lying to himself and insisting he felt fine, Mark had to face the fact that his time on the field and in the cage had caused potentially irreparable damage inside his skull.

Tired of throwing in the towel when things get difficult, Mark committed to make his recovery an adventure in health, happiness, and self-discovery. And now he's sharing his journey, research, and joy with you, hoping that you, too, can recover and walk out of the darkness. A powerful balance of scientific fact and personal triumph, this testament to the strength of the human spirit is impossible to put down.

Try Not to Die: In the Wizard's Tower

Mark and Michael Sage Ricci bring the first fantasy Try Not to Die. Scheduled for release late 2021.

Try Not to Die: Super High

Mark and Steve Montgomery team up to bring the Try Not to Die series to Florida. Become a young competitive sharpshooter and enjoy a night out in Miami. Just don't get bit by any of the bath salt people. Scheduled for release early 2022.

Tales of the Blessed and Broken: The Early Years

A collection of 27 short stories set in the *Tales of the Blessed and Broken* world. Take a look at the childhoods of three protagonists from the 5-book series: Heimdall, Lucas, and Vincent. Scheduled for release early 2022.

ABOUT THE AUTHOR

Mark Tullius is the author of *Unlocking the Cage, Ain't No Messiah, Twisted Reunion, 25 Perfect Days, Brightside,* and the creator of the *Try Not to Die* series. Mark resides in Southern California with his wife and two children.

To follow and connect with Mark you can click: https://youcanfollow.me/MarkTullius

To sign up for Mark's no-spam newsletter go to his website: https://www.marktullius.com/

Podcast - https://viciouswhispers.podbean.com
Goodreads - https://bit.ly/2EDs2zV
Website - www.MarkTullius.com
Instagram - @author_mark_tullius
Facebook   –
http://www.facebook.com/AuthorMarkTullius
Twitter - https://twitter.com/MarkTullius
YouTube – http://www.youtube.com/MarkTullius

To hear free audiobooks and listen to Mark's weekly rant, be sure to look for his new podcast, *Vicious Whispers with Mark Tullius* which you can find on YouTube, iTunes, iHeart radio, Spotify, Stitcher and other places podcasts are played.

https://viciouswhispers.podbean.com

Your Free Book is Waiting

Three short horror stories and one piece of nonfiction by Mark Tullius, one of the hardest-hitting authors around. The tales are bound to leave you more than a touch unsettled.

Get to know:

- an overweight father ignored by his family and paying the ultimate and unexpected price for his sins

- a gang member breaking into a neighborhood church despite the nagging feeling that something about the situation is desperately wrong

- a cameraman who finds himself in a hopeless situation after his involvement in exposing a sex trafficking ring

- the aging author paying the price for a reckless past, now doing all he can to repair his brain

These shocking stories will leave you wanting more.
Get a free copy of this collection.
Morsels of Mayhem: An Unsettling Appetizer here:
https://www.marktullius.com/free-book-is-waiting

CPSIA information can be obtained
at www.ICGtesting.com
Printed in the USA
LVHW101949261222
735917LV00004B/263